Silence in daffodils

Anuj Kumar

For the parts of us that learned to survive quietly—
and for the courage it takes to unlearn that silence.

Author's Note

This book lives at the intersection of story and psychology. While the characters and events are fictional, the emotional patterns explored here are very real.

Attachment shapes how we love, fear, withdraw, pursue, and connect—and most of us live these patterns long before we understand them. This is not a clinical guide, nor a diagnosis. It is an invitation: to notice, to reflect, and to understand how early emotional experiences echo into adult relationships.

If you recognize yourself in these pages, know that recognition is not a flaw—it is the beginning of awareness. Healing does not begin with blame. It begins with understanding.

— Anuj Kumar

Introduction

Have you ever found yourself caught in the same kind of relationship over and over again? Perhaps you've felt an overwhelming closeness with someone, only to sense them pulling away the moment you needed them most. Or maybe you've noticed yourself withdrawing emotionally, even while longing deeply for connection. These patterns are not random. They are not accidents. They are echoes of something older and deeper—an emotional blueprint formed long before we had the words to understand what we were feeling.

This book is about that blueprint. It explores attachment—the quiet force that shapes how we love, connect, and cope with closeness and distance. It is about the emotional map we inherit in childhood and carry, often unknowingly, into every friendship, romance, and heartbreak we experience.

Attachment theory is not a concept confined to psychology textbooks. It is lived reality—woven into our most tender memories and intimate moments. From our earliest days, the way caregivers responded to our cries, our needs, and our hunger for safety shaped our nervous systems. These early interactions taught us whether love feels safe or dangerous, whether closeness brings comfort or risk, and whether we are worthy of being seen, held, and cherished.

Over time, these experiences form what psychologists call attachment styles, and they often surface in adulthood with surprising intensity. Yet most of us don't realize we're living by them. We simply sense that something feels off. We feel too much or too little. We crave closeness or shut down when intimacy deepens. We cling, withdraw, disappear, pursue—and repeat.

In this book, we will explore six primary attachment styles:

- Secure – The foundation of healthy relationships. Those with a secure style are comfortable with intimacy, resilient during conflict, and able to give and receive love freely.

- Anxious – Deeply invested in relationships but often burdened by fear of abandonment. Emotional highs and lows and a constant need for reassurance can make love feel unstable.

- Dismissive-Avoidant – Highly independent and emotionally distant. Often perceived as aloof, they prioritize self-sufficiency and avoid deep emotional vulnerability.

- Fearful-Avoidant – A complex blend of anxiety and avoidance. These individuals crave closeness yet fear it, often caught in painful push–pull dynamics.

- Disorganized – Frequently rooted in trauma, this style lacks a consistent strategy for connection. Relationships are marked by confusion, intensity, and unpredictability.

- Narcissistic – While not a traditional attachment style, narcissistic patterns often emerge from profound attachment disruptions. Beneath the façade of confidence and control is often a deeply unseen child longing for validation.

Each of these styles carries its own emotional triggers, behaviors, and relational patterns. Most importantly, each originates from how we learned to survive emotionally. These patterns are not flaws. They are intelligent adaptations. They once protected us. But what kept us safe as children can quietly become a barrier in our adult lives—especially in our most intimate relationships.

This book is a deep exploration of these emotional patterns. Together, we will examine where attachment styles originate, how they appear in everyday relationships—from texting habits to arguments to breakups—why they are so difficult to change, and how healing can begin, one layer at a time.

But this book is not just a guide. It is a story—a human one. It unfolds through the lives of two people who didn't simply love each other; they collided. Their connection was intense, intoxicating, and at times deeply painful. It was shaped not just by personality or circumstance, but by emotional maps drawn long before they met—in the quiet, formative spaces of childhood.

This is a story of love entangled with mental health struggles. Of connection that feels like salvation one moment and suffocation the next. Of trying to love someone while barely holding yourself together. It is about two people who couldn't seem to stay away from each other—or remain whole when they were together.

As you follow their journey, you may begin to recognize your own. The anxious waiting for a reply. The relief when it finally arrives. The cold silences. The emotional shutdowns. The longing for safety paired with the fear of intimacy. These are not personal failures. They are shared human experiences, rooted in early emotional learning.

Throughout the book, you'll encounter reflective questions, journal prompts, and psychological insights—gentle invitations to pause, turn inward, and explore your own patterns with curiosity rather than judgment. The aim is not to label or pathologize, but to bring these patterns into the light—where they can be seen, understood, and softened.

Because here is the truth: you are not broken. You adapted. And once you understand the why behind your emotional reactions, you can begin to write a different story—one where connection feels safer, love feels steadier, and you become your own secure base.

So whether you are in the middle of a complicated relationship, healing from a painful ending, or simply trying to understand yourself more deeply, this book is for you.

How will we do this? By telling the story of two individuals bound by their mental health struggles—learning how difficult it can be to navigate life together, and how painful it can be to survive apart.

Reflection

Understanding attachment is not about revisiting the past to assign blame—it is about reclaiming choice. When you recognize the patterns guiding your emotions and relationships, you gain the power to respond rather than react, to connect without fear, and to build love from awareness instead of survival.

Chapter 1

The city buzzed with life as Columbia University opened its doors to the incoming freshman class that summer. Aarav, a boy from a sprawling metropolis like Mumbai, stepped down from the airport shuttle into a world that felt entirely unfamiliar. The air was crisp, laced with the scent of spring leaves and blooming flowers. He boarded another bus straight to campus, his thoughts racing as fast as the city around him. Slightly disoriented, he passed through the campus gates, searching for his marketing class while a sea of students moved confidently around him, each absorbed in their own rhythm. His arrival had been delayed by a cancelled flight, and now he hurried across the grounds, his suitcase clattering along the cobblestone path. The sound was rhythmic and oddly comforting—like a heartbeat anchoring him in this new place. As he walked, his mind wandered to what lay ahead: new friendships, unfamiliar experiences, and the long-awaited freedom from the watchful eyes of his family back home.

"Aarav, right?" a voice broke through his thoughts.

He turned to see a tall guy with curly hair and a warm, welcoming smile, his hand already extended.

"Yeah, that's me," Aarav replied, shaking hands with his dorm roommate, Mark.

"Welcome to Grandview! Let me show you around," Mark said, effortlessly lifting Aarav's suitcase and leading him toward the dorm building.

They walked through the residence halls and across campus, Mark pointing out the historic library and student unions along the way. Aarav took it all in—the architecture, the energy, the quiet confidence with which everyone seemed to belong. Beneath his excitement lingered a soft ache of homesickness. He felt grounded and restless at once, aware that there was so much ahead of him, yet none of it was certain. Still, he reminded himself of the promise he had made to his mother—to give himself the world. This place was about to become home for the next few years, and he felt ready to claim it.

Chapter 2

B ack in the dorm room, Mark introduced him to a few more people, all of them warm and eager to talk. Their friendliness eased Aarav's nerves even further. As the evening settled in, he found himself sitting on a couch, flipping through orientation brochures, when a sudden burst of laughter shifted the energy in the room. He looked up to see a group of girls walking in, their presence instantly filling the space.

Her heels tapped against the wooden floor, drawing every eye toward her. Auburn hair cascaded down her shoulders, lips the color of ripe cherries, and a laugh that seemed to occupy the entire room before she even spoke. She stood there with her girlfriends, radiant and unapologetically present.

"Come on now, Aimee, we've been waiting," Mark called out.

"Aimee," Aarav repeated silently. The name lingered with unexpected weight. He felt drawn to her in a way that startled him—almost embarrassed him. It sounded cliché, the idea of being so affected at first sight. And yet, life had a way of unfolding in moments you never see coming. She was European, he quickly gathered from her accent, and she carried a confidence that was both intriguing and slightly intimidating.

"Hey there, new guy," Aimee said with a playful smile, her eyes locking onto his. "First-day jitters?"

"Something like that," Aarav replied with a nervous chuckle, warmth creeping into his face. "Just getting used to everything here."

She nodded, her expression softening. "It can be overwhelming at first—but trust me, you'll love it here."

Their conversation flowed with surprising ease, drifting between culture, travel, and the shared thrill of being somewhere new. Aarav found himself captivated by her stories of life in Paris and her reasons for choosing to study abroad in America. Neither of them could name it yet, but something had quietly begun—a connection they didn't fully understand, yet both instinctively felt.

As the night stretched on, Aarav and Aimee continued sharing jokes, laughter, and the discovery of how much they had in common. With her, Aarav felt an unfamiliar sense of ease—one that exhilarated him even as it unsettled something deep within. Weeks passed almost without notice. They spent countless hours together after classes, meeting whenever they could. In Mumbai, Aarav's relationships had often been shaped by a need for reassurance and closeness—patterns that eventually pushed people away. With Aimee, things felt different. She seemed to understand his desire for connection without judgment, offering a sense of security he had never truly known.

Reflection

Beginnings often feel gentle and full of promise, but beneath that ease, patterns are already forming. What feels like comfort and chemistry can also be the quiet alignment of unmet needs—drawing two people together before either understands what they are truly seeking.

Chapter 3

In Aarav's mind, he was growing attached to Aimee far more quickly than he cared to admit. He had no real sense of how she felt—whether she shared even a fraction of what stirred inside him. To Aimee, however, Aarav felt like a breath of fresh air. She admired his enthusiasm for life, his ability to find meaning in ordinary moments, and his openness toward vulnerability. Still, an unshakable fear lingered beneath her warmth. Her avoidant attachment often compelled her to retreat from emotional closeness—a defense that had once protected her heart but had also kept her isolated from deeper bonds. Their connection became a delicate dance, a quiet negotiation between Aarav's longing for closeness and Aimee's instinct to pull away. Despite the tension, they found comfort in each other's presence, a temporary sanctuary from the noise of the world.

One October evening, they wandered down Fifth Avenue with mint chocolate chip gelatos in hand—Aimee's favorite, which had quickly become Aarav's ritual too. The setting sun painted the sky in soft oranges and pinks, leaves rustling gently as if the city itself had paused to watch them pass.

"Aimee, have you ever thought about what it really means to connect with someone?" Aarav asked, his voice barely above a whisper.

She stopped and looked out toward the shimmering water, her expression thoughtful, as though the answer wasn't easily accessible.

"I think it's about letting someone in," she said finally, meeting his gaze. "Allowing them to see the parts of you you usually keep hidden."

Aarav felt the weight of her words settle deep within him. He wanted to be that person for her—the one she could trust, the one she could lean on. Yet he sensed the invisible barriers between them, shaped by attachment patterns neither of them fully understood yet. As they made their way back toward the university, Aarav realized that their different approaches to closeness would be complex to navigate. Still, he was willing to try—even if it meant confronting his own insecurities and fears.

Their cultural differences added yet another layer to their unfolding story, sometimes intriguing, sometimes challenging. Aarav's upbringing in a traditional Indian family had instilled in him values of loyalty, respect, and deep familial bonds. Aimee, raised in a more liberal European environment, had grown up celebrating independence and self-expression. One weekend, after submitting assignments, Aarav suggested they try something different—an Indian restaurant. Aimee hesitated briefly, then agreed, her spontaneous side winning out.

Chapter 4

The moment they stepped inside, familiar aromas wrapped around Aarav, stirring a sharp wave of homesickness. He was pulled from his thoughts when Aimee clutched his arm. "There—let's sit by the window. I like watching people on the street," she said. They took the table, and Aarav ordered a generous spread of his favorite dishes—kebabs, naan, and rich chicken gravies. When the food arrived, he eagerly dug in. Aimee watched him with quiet amusement, charmed by the unfiltered joy on his face. She reached out and gently wiped a stray smudge from beneath his lip. Startled, Aarav flushed and quickly looked away, pretending not to notice. When Aimee took her first bite, she laughed through watering eyes. "I think you're trying to kill me with this heat!"

"It's called flavor," Aarav teased, a playful glint in his eyes. "You Europeans don't know what you're missing."

After dinner, Aimee checked the time. "I should head back—papers to finish. Let's make this quick." As they walked, a light drizzle began, soon turning into a steady downpour. Autumn rain had its own way of transforming New York. Cars sped past, water splashing onto the sidewalks. Instinctively, Aarav pulled Aimee closer to the safer edge, his grip firm, unwilling to let go. For a suspended moment, everything seemed to go quiet. Aimee looked at him with an expression he couldn't yet decipher. All he could see were her brown eyes, steady and searching. Is this love? he wondered. The moment broke as she gently pulled her hand away. Aarav felt a flicker of embarrassment, but they continued walking.

"Have you always been this way, Aarav?" she asked.

"What way?"

"There's more to you than meets the eye," she said with a grin. "So much more. One day I'll figure it out—I promise. No mystery escapes me."

In the days that followed, life resumed its usual rhythm until excitement began building around Harper's Halloween party—the party everyone on campus talked about, the one that felt impossible to miss.

Reflection

When two people want closeness in different ways, affection can feel both comforting and confusing. Attraction grows easily in moments of warmth, but the real tension lives in the space between approach and retreat—where unspoken fears quietly shape what love is allowed to become.

Chapter 5

Aarav had been texting Aimee regularly. She replied—always—but on her own time. In person, she felt warm, present, almost intimate; through text, she felt distant, unfamiliar. At times, Aarav wondered if he was speaking to two different versions of the same person. He dissected every message, every pause, searching for meaning between the lines even when there was none to be found. His anxiety deepened as his attachment grew. He woke to his alarm sweating beneath heavy blankets, his first instinct always the same—reach for his phone and check if Aimee had texted. It became routine. After classes, when they met, he hid it well, wearing ease like armor. Around her, when she listened and laughed and seemed wholly present, he let himself relax. But once he was back in his dorm, the cycle returned—scrolling through old messages, refreshing screens, every notification igniting hope only to extinguish it moments later. How could someone feel so close in person and so far away in absence? The question gnawed at him nightly. He replayed every interaction, blamed himself for imagined missteps, and denied how deeply this anxious attachment was affecting him. This wasn't new—but it was stronger, heavier, more consuming than before. This time felt serious. The feelings, the uncertainty, the endless questions about them—or whether them even existed.

Then came the night of Harper's party. The moment Aimee arrived with her friends, the room seemed to turn toward her. Her dark, glossy hair cascaded down her back, catching the light with every movement. She wore a shimmering black dress, sequins scattering reflections like a thousand tiny mirrors. Confidence and mischief sparkled in her eyes, drawing attention without effort.

When the DJ slid into a popular remix, Aimee's friends pulled her onto the dance floor. The music surged through her, syncing with her heartbeat. She moved with fluid grace—effortless, magnetic. Her feet traced the beat with precision, arms carving the air as though the rhythm belonged to her alone. It was a seamless blend of contemporary flow and hip-hop edge, unmistakably her.

The crowd slowed, mesmerized. It felt as though the music was moving through her, guiding each step with instinctive certainty. A loose circle formed, granting her space. She spun, hair fanning out like a halo, eyes closed, a serene smile softening her face as she surrendered fully to the moment. Cheers erupted. Applause followed. People joined in, inhibitions dissolving as the room pulsed with shared energy. In that instant, Aimee became the heart of the party—confident, luminous, alive. As the beat shifted electronic, she adapted effortlessly, locking eyes with friends and drawing them into an impromptu circle. Laughter rang out. Camaraderie took hold. When the song peaked, she finished with a dramatic flourish that left the room breathless. Applause thundered. She bowed playfully, grinning as compliments poured in. Dancing was her language—the way she expressed what words could not—and tonight she shared it freely, leaving an imprint that lingered.

As the night wore on, Aimee drifted from group to group, talking and dancing, her presence weaving unity through the house. Amid flashing lights and pulsing music, she felt exhilarated, entirely in her element. Eventually, the crowd's attention scattered, the party splintering into smaller moments as the music continued its steady thrum.

Reflection

Anxious attachment feeds on distance and ambiguity, turning silence into stories and pauses into proof. When connection feels inconsistent, the mind searches for certainty—but what it often finds instead is exhaustion, confusion, and the quiet erosion of self-trust.

Chapter 6

The party was in full swing inside the sprawling mansion owned by Harper Kane. A tall, striking senior with a reputation as large as his bank account, Harper was infamous for hosting nights that bled into dawn. His presence carried equal parts excitement and unease; he was popular, but often for the wrong reasons. Harper thrived on chaos, wearing his notoriety with a grin that never quite reached his eyes. His father, a powerful real estate tycoon, owned the lavish mansion that had become the unofficial epicenter of campus excess. Rumors followed Harper everywhere—reckless adventures, whispered scandals, and a charm so effortless it was almost dangerous. The mansion itself, with its vast rooms and opulent décor, felt like the perfect stage for indulgence—a place where secrets were exchanged and illusions quietly unraveled.

As Harper scanned the dance floor, his attention landed on Aimee. She still held the room's energy, her laughter rising above the noise as she stood with her friends, the afterglow of her performance lingering around her. Something about her pulled him in. Her presence was magnetic, luminous against the dim lighting. He watched her brush her hair back, cheeks flushed with exhilaration, and felt an undeniable urge to approach. With practiced confidence, drink in hand and a charming smile ready, Harper made his way through the crowd. Heads turned instinctively—Harper Kane rarely went unnoticed.

As he reached her, Aimee's friends subtly shifted aside. She looked up, momentarily surprised, curiosity quickly replacing it.

"Aimee, right?" Harper said smoothly. "That dancing—everyone's talking about it."

She smiled, pride tempered by modesty. "Thanks. I didn't realize I had an audience."

Harper chuckled. "Trust me, you did. It's rare to see real talent at parties like this."

There was a glint of mischief in his eyes, and Aimee felt a flicker of excitement. She knew his reputation—everyone did—but in that moment, his charm was difficult to resist.

"You're flattering me," she replied lightly. "But I'm sure you're used to being the center of attention yourself."

"Maybe," Harper said, raising an eyebrow, "but tonight's about you. How about we show them what real dancing looks like?"

He extended his hand—part invitation, part challenge. The crowd seemed to pause, anticipation thick in the air. Aimee hesitated, aware of the watching eyes and the inevitable gossip that would follow. Still, the thrill of the unknown tugged at her. With a confident nod, she placed her hand in his, letting him lead her back onto the dance floor. The crowd parted instinctively, murmurs trailing behind them.

As the music shifted to a seductive beat, Aimee felt it surge through her, her body syncing effortlessly. Harper surprised her—he moved with skill and awareness, keeping a careful balance between flirtation and restraint. Together, they danced in seamless harmony, their chemistry unmistakable. It was a wordless exchange, a charged push and pull that captivated the room. Harper spun her with practiced ease, and adrenaline flooded Aimee—excitement threaded with danger, quickening her pulse.

For a moment, the rest of the party disappeared. The room blurred into background noise as the music and their shared rhythm took over. When the song slowed, Harper drew her closer, their bodies swaying in sync, the air between them heavy with unspoken tension. She felt alive, unburdened, caught in the glow of the moment.

Unseen by her, Aarav stood at the edge of the room, his fingers clenched tightly around his drink. He had arrived earlier, hoping to surprise Aimee, to spend the night with her. What he witnessed instead sent a sharp surge of jealousy and anger through him. His deep blue eyes stayed fixed on the dance floor as Aimee and Harper moved as though no one else existed. When Harper leaned in to whisper something that made her laugh—a sound Aarav felt should have belonged to him—it cut deeper than he expected.

A storm churned inside Aarav. Betrayal, insecurity, and fear collided in his chest, each emotion feeding the next. He had always trusted Aimee, believed in their connection and the quiet bond they were building. But seeing her in Harper's arms—a man infamous for recklessness—felt like a blow he hadn't prepared for. The image lodged itself painfully in his mind, leaving him questioning everything he thought he understood.

Reflection

Attraction doesn't always threaten a relationship—uncertainty does. When closeness feels fragile, the sight of another person stepping into that space can awaken fear, jealousy, and a desperate need for reassurance, revealing how deeply attachment is tied to our sense of emotional safety.

Chapter 7

Aarav's grip tightened around his drink as he tried to make sense of what he was witnessing. He had always trusted Aimee—believed in the connection they were building, in the quiet bond that felt real and meaningful to him. But watching her with Harper, seeing the ease and chemistry between them, cracked that certainty wide open. Doubt crept in where trust had lived.

The rational part of his mind urged him to walk away, to leave the party and allow Aimee her night. But the jealousy burning inside him refused to be quiet. It clawed at him, demanding action, demanding that he reclaim what he believed was slipping from his grasp. As the music pulsed on, his eyes never left the dance floor. With every synchronized movement between Aimee and Harper, the distance between Aarav and her seemed to widen—a gap he felt powerless to cross, one that threatened to consume him.

As the song reached its peak, Aimee, caught in the intensity of the moment, leaned closer to Harper. The world around them dissolved into noise and blur, leaving only charged silence and proximity. Harper's gaze held hers, intent and unflinching. Before she could fully register what was happening, their lips met in a brief, electrifying kiss. It was sudden and overwhelming—a spark that left Aimee breathless, stunned by the rush of emotion it ignited.

For Aarav, watching from the shadows, the kiss was the breaking point. The final thread of self-control snapped. Rage surged through him, sharp and uncontainable. Without thinking, he pushed through the crowd, driven by instinct rather than reason. He reached Harper just as the kiss ended and shoved him with all his strength.

Gasps rippled through the crowd as Harper stumbled backward, arms flailing before he toppled into the pool with a loud splash. Water erupted in all directions, soaking those nearby. The music faltered, then stopped altogether, a stunned silence settling over the party as all eyes turned toward the chaos.

Aimee stood frozen for a heartbeat, shock written across her face—anger and confusion colliding at once. Then she turned and stormed away, pushing through the stunned onlookers. Laughter and hoots rose behind her as disbelief spread—no one could quite grasp what a freshman had just done to Harper Kane. Aarav himself seemed momentarily paralyzed before snapping back into motion and chasing after her.

Outside, the air had turned cold. Aimee walked quickly, clutching her sweatshirt tighter around herself. She could hear Aarav calling her name, but she didn't slow down. When he finally caught up and grabbed her arm, she spun around sharply.

"Ouch—you're hurting me!" she shouted, anger flaring.

"I—I'm sorry. I didn't mean to. I just didn't want you to think—"

"Think what, Aarav?" she cut in. "Is there any way you can explain what you just did? Why you did it?"

"No," he said quietly, panic rising. "I don't think you're ready for that answer yet."

"What is it? Try me."

The words spilled out of him then—raw and unfiltered. How hard it was to see her with someone else. How scared he felt. How confusing it was when she felt distant over text but warm in person. How he waited for her replies, how the silence ate at him.

"What do you want me to do?" Aimee interrupted, her voice sharp. "Is that it? Is that why you're acting like this?"

Aarav's face fell. He had no answer.

"Thought so," she said quietly. "I've liked being around you, Aarav. I've liked spending time with you. But I don't know what you expect from me. I don't like feeling as if you're clinging to me. I can't change who I am. If you're okay with me just being me, then we can talk."

"Or?" he asked softly.

"Or not tonight," she said firmly. "Let me sleep on it. We'll already have enough to deal with tomorrow after what you pulled."

He asked if he could walk her back to her dorm. After a pause, she agreed—hesitant, guarded. They walked in silence. After leaving her at the door, Aarav returned to his own dorm alone, his thoughts heavy and relentless. He replayed everything, questioning where he had lost control, why this part of him kept overpowering reason. He wanted to be calm, to let things unfold naturally. But anxiety had a way of resurfacing when least expected—unhealed pieces carried quietly until they erupted.

That night, Aarav made a promise to himself: to take responsibility for his emotions, to steady his center, to stop letting fear dictate his actions—even if he didn't yet know how.

Reflection

When fear of loss overtakes trust, emotions can hijack reason and turn love into panic. Unhealed anxiety doesn't ask for permission—it demands control. Real growth begins not with grand apologies or promises, but with the quiet, difficult work of learning to sit with fear without letting it decide who we become.

Chapter 8

The next morning arrived heavy with questions as Aarav stepped back through the university gates. Eyes followed him everywhere. Whispers lingered in the air. He felt like a spectacle, an unspoken headline everyone had already read. Keeping his head down, he moved quickly, avoiding eye contact—until a sudden chill ran down his spine. He looked up to see Harper walking toward him, his stride sharp, unmistakably hostile. Each step closed the distance faster than Aarav could process.

Before he could react, Harper's fist connected with his face. Aarav hit the ground hard, his head spinning as the world tilted. He stared up at the sky above the campus, light blurring, dizziness creeping in.

"You're bleeding—get up, Aarav. What the hell was that, Harper?"

A familiar hand gripped his, pulling him up. It was Aimee. She pressed a handkerchief to his nose, her face tight with worry, hair disheveled as she steadied him. Inexplicably, Aarav smiled.

"I cannot believe you're smiling right now," she snapped. "Are you stupid? You just got hit. You're bleeding."

"You came," he said softly. "You held me up. You care, Aimee. That's all I needed to know."

"Of course I care," she replied, exasperated. "Haven't I made that clear?"

She walked him to the infirmary, stayed beside him as the doctor checked his vitals and treated the injury. When she helped him lie back, he held her hand, his voice barely audible.

"You're not leaving, are you?"

"No," she said quietly. "I'm right here. As long as you need me to."

Her reassurance sank deeper than she realized. And now that he had felt it, Aarav wasn't ready to let go.

The pain medication knocked him out for hours. When he opened his eyes, the sterile scent of the infirmary was softened by something familiar—vanilla. Aimee sat curled up on the nearby sofa, half asleep.

"Aimee... what are you doing here?"

"I guess I fell asleep," she said, blinking awake. "How are you feeling? Still hurting?"

"I think I'm better now," he said. "Now that you're here."

"Let's get you home."

She helped him back to his dorm room. Aarav barely spoke. Shame weighed heavily on him, and he couldn't bring himself to meet her eyes. She left without a word.

Before that night, their lives had moved in a shared rhythm—late nights studying, meals at the crowded cafeteria, quiet familiarity born of proximity. But after the incident, something shifted.

An invisible wall rose between them, one neither knew how to dismantle. Conversations that once flowed effortlessly now stalled. Comfort was replaced by silence.

They still crossed paths daily—brief nods in hallways, awkward smiles exchanged in passing. Friends noticed the change but stayed silent, unsure of what had fractured the closeness between them. Aimee felt the distance more than she admitted. She missed Aarav—the way he made her laugh, the way he seemed to understand her without words. Yet each time she thought of reaching out, fear held her back, whispering that whatever had broken might not be repairable.

One weekend, the university organized a group hike through a nearby forest. Aimee signed up despite her hesitation—she had always loved the outdoors. Seeing Aarav's name on the list didn't surprise her, but it unsettled her. As they gathered at the trailhead, a quiet sense lingered that this day might shift something.

They set off early, the air crisp with autumn promise. Sunlight filtered through the trees in golden streaks as the trail wound through dense woods. Aimee walked near the middle of the group, her steps falling into rhythm with the crunch of leaves beneath her boots. Aarav was farther ahead, laughing with friends. She kept her distance.

As the hike stretched on, the group thinned—some moving faster, others lagging behind. Eventually, Aimee found herself alone on the trail, surrounded by stillness broken only by her breath and the call of distant birds. She welcomed the solitude. It gave her space to think, to sit with the emotions she'd been carrying without distraction.

Reflection

Moments of rupture don't always end relationships—they reveal what lies beneath them. When guilt, fear, and longing collide, distance can feel safer than honesty. Yet it's often in quiet, unguarded spaces—away from crowds and noise—that the truth finally finds room to surface.

Chapter 9

As Aimee rounded a bend in the trail, a sudden rustle broke the stillness. She froze, her heart slamming hard against her ribs. The sound was too heavy, too deliberate to belong to an animal. She peered into the shadows just beyond the path and caught a flicker of movement—someone, or something, concealed among the trees.

Her thoughts spiraled. Stories she'd heard surfaced unbidden—rumors of Harper, the student expelled the previous year after a series of disturbing incidents. Whispers that he hadn't truly left campus. A cold wave of fear crept up her spine as she took a cautious step back, eyes scanning the dense woods.

Without warning, a figure burst from the underbrush. Aimee barely had time to gasp before she was tackled to the ground. Panic consumed her as she struggled beneath the sudden weight, the forest floor cold and unforgiving beneath her. When she managed to focus, she saw his face twisted with rage.

Harper.

A manic grin spread across his features. "You shouldn't have come here alone, Aimee," he hissed, malice dripping from every word. "You're just like the others—easy to corner, easy to break."

Her heart thundered in her ears as she fought to push him away, but he was stronger. The realization that she was truly in danger sent terror coursing through her body.

Then a voice cut through the chaos.

"Get off her!"

Aarav's shout echoed through the trees, fierce and unrestrained. In an instant, he was there—grabbing Harper by the shoulders and yanking him away with a force Aimee didn't know he possessed. Harper stumbled, barely regaining his footing before Aarav struck him, his fist connecting hard with Harper's jaw.

Aimee scrambled to her feet, breath ragged, as she watched the two men crash to the ground. Harper fought wildly, but Aarav's determination was unyielding. He moved with a singular purpose—to protect her. After a brutal struggle, Aarav managed to pin Harper down.

"Stay away from her!" Aarav shouted, his voice raw with fury. "If you ever come near Aimee again, you'll regret it."

Harper spat in defiance, but fear flickered unmistakably in his eyes. Aarav tightened his grip just long enough to make his message clear. Then he shoved Harper toward the trail.

"Get out of here."

After a tense moment, Harper staggered away, disappearing into the woods, his bravado dissolved.

Silence followed—thick and heavy. Aimee stood trembling, adrenaline still surging through her veins. Aarav turned to her, his anger gone, replaced by unmistakable concern. His hands hovered, then gently steadied her arms as he checked for injuries.

"Aimee... are you okay?" he asked softly.

She nodded, words caught in her throat. The warmth of his touch grounded her, anchoring her back into safety. Their eyes met, and for a brief moment, the distance that had separated them for weeks seemed to vanish. Worry lingered in his gaze—along with something deeper, something he could no longer hide.

"I'm sorry," he said quietly. "I should've been there sooner. I shouldn't have let you walk alone."

"It's not your fault," she replied, her voice finally steadying. "You saved me."

Emotion flickered across his face, and before either of them could think twice, he pulled her into his arms. Aimee exhaled a breath she hadn't realized she'd been holding and wrapped herself around him, pressing her face into his shoulder. The world receded. For the first time in weeks, the tension dissolved, replaced by a warmth she had missed more than she wanted to admit.

When they finally pulled apart, Aarav looked at her as if he were about to say something important.

"Aimee, I—"

A low rumble interrupted him. Fat drops of rain began to fall, soaking through them within seconds. Aarav laughed softly, shaking his head as he wiped rain from his face.

"Of course it would rain now."

Despite everything, Aimee smiled. "We should find shelter."

Aarav took her hand without hesitation. "There's a lake nearby. A small cabin—we can wait it out there."

They set off together, rain turning the trail slick beneath their feet. Aimee's thoughts were still racing, but with Aarav's hand firmly in hers, a sense of calm settled over her—steady, grounding, and unfamiliar in the best way.

Reflection

Crisis has a way of stripping away pretense. In moments of real danger, fear gives way to instinct, and what remains is truth—who shows up, who protects, and who stays. Sometimes safety doesn't come from certainty or control, but from realizing you're not alone when it matters most.

Chapter 10

The lake came into view just as the rain intensified, the water churning beneath the force of the storm. Aarav guided Aimee toward a small cabin tucked among the trees. It was old—likely abandoned—but it offered refuge from the downpour. They slipped inside, shaking off the rain as best they could.

The cabin was dim, lit only by narrow windows along the walls. Aarav found an old lantern and coaxed it to life, its warm glow softening the space. In one corner stood a small fireplace. He gathered the dry wood stacked beside it and soon had a fire crackling, warmth slowly filling the room.

Aimee watched him, her pulse still racing from the adrenaline, now intertwined with something else—an attraction she had tried to ignore for far too long. In the quiet of the cabin, with the storm raging outside, denial felt impossible. When Aarav turned to her, his expression serious, she felt the weight of the moment settle between them.

"You're sure you're okay?" he asked, searching her face.

"I am," she said, stepping closer. "Because of you."

He hesitated, running a hand through his damp hair. "I don't want to lose you."

Her breath caught. "You haven't," she replied softly. "But I feel like I've been losing you."

He closed his eyes briefly, then met her gaze again, vulnerability laid bare. "I've been scared," he admitted. "Scared of what I feel for you. Scared that if I get too close, I'll ruin everything."

"I've been scared too," Aimee whispered, resting her hand on his arm. "But what I feel is real. And I think it's time we stop running."

He didn't answer with words. He closed the distance and kissed her—gentle, certain, and full of everything left unsaid. Aimee kissed him back, fear dissolving into warmth as the weeks of confusion fell away. The storm outside faded into insignificance. When they finally parted, breathless, Aarav rested his forehead against hers.

"I've wanted to do that for so long," he said, voice trembling.

"Me too," she whispered, relief and joy blurring together.

They sat by the fire as the night stretched on, shadows dancing on the walls while rain drummed steadily on the roof. They spoke honestly—of insecurities, fears, and the distance that had grown between them. Aarav shared the quiet doubts that had driven his anxiety; Aimee spoke of her fear of closeness and the walls she built to feel safe. With every confession, the space between them softened, threads of understanding knitting something steadier in place.

By dawn, the storm had eased. They stepped outside and sat by the lake as the sky bloomed with soft oranges and pinks, the water reflecting the morning like a watercolor. The world felt washed clean. Aarav took her hand, his grip sure.

"I don't want to be apart anymore," he said. "I want to be with you. For real."

"I want that too," Aimee replied. "No more running. No more hiding."

He pulled her close as the sun rose, warmth settling between them. The chaos of the night—fear, distance, misunderstanding—receded like the storm itself. In the stillness of morning, with the lake mirroring their calm, they found each other again, steadier and more certain than before, ready to write what came next together.

Reflection

Reconnection doesn't arrive through perfection—it arrives through honesty. When fear is named and vulnerability is met with presence, attachment begins to heal. What feels like a dramatic turning point is often a quiet decision: to stop running, to stay, and to choose each other with clarity rather than fear.

Chapter 11

The walk back to their dorms was the most beautiful morning Aarav could remember. He kept smiling, glancing at Aimee, her hand warm in his, as if he still couldn't quite believe this was real. Each time he tugged her a little closer, her cheeks flushed, and the sight made his heart swell. When they reached the dorms, reality gently pulled them apart—separate hallways, separate doors.

Before letting go, Aarav leaned in and kissed her softly. "Morning, baby. Have a good day. I'll see you at the uni."

Aimee's cheeks burned at the word baby, butterflies rising in a way she had never known before. She had always been reserved—quiet, composed, a little intimidating even—but she also knew how to live fully. And lately, she could feel herself changing, opening, all because of Aarav. She went to her room, showered, got ready, and headed out, heart light and hopeful.

The moment she stepped onto campus, the weight of reality returned. Harper. The thought made her stomach tighten. Whatever they had shared the night before didn't erase the consequences waiting for them. She scanned the crowd nervously—until Aarav appeared, slipping his hand into hers without hesitation. Relief washed over her.

"Hey babe," he teased. "It's only been one night and you're already tired of me?"

"No," she said quickly. "It's just... Harper. I don't know what's coming, and I'm scared."

"Don't be," Aarav replied calmly. "After last night, I don't think he'll try anything. And if he does, you go to the authorities. You call him out."

"But he's powerful."

"The truth always outlasts power," Aarav said gently. "My naanu used to say that."

"Your who?"

He laughed. "My grandfather. I spent most of my childhood with him. He lives near Nashik."

The growing hum of campus life swallowed the moment as students rushed past, preparing for the day. Aarav squeezed her hand and smiled. "Come on. We'll get through today together."

Aimee nodded, grateful. They walked through campus side by side, their closeness obvious to anyone who noticed. Classes blurred into conversations, laughter, and stolen moments, the fear of Harper never quite disappearing—but softened by Aarav's steady presence.

As days passed, their bond deepened into something comfortable and reassuring. University stress faded into the background as they built small rituals—late-night study sessions punctuated by laughter, quick kisses between lectures, long conversations that stretched into the early hours. One afternoon, bathed in warm sunlight, Aarav suggested returning to the lake. The idea felt both calming and symbolic, and Aimee agreed without hesitation.

The hike was refreshing, the trail winding through lush greenery. Aarav talked animatedly, pointing out small details, sharing stories. Aimee found herself smiling more easily, her fears momentarily quiet. When they reached the lake, it shimmered just as it had before. Aarav spread a blanket, and they shared a simple picnic, laughter echoing across the still water. When he tucked a loose strand of hair behind her ear, the intimacy of the gesture made her heart ache in the best way. Their connection was no longer just excitement—it was becoming something deeper, steadier.

Still, Harper lingered at the edges of her thoughts, an unease she couldn't entirely silence. Days passed in romantic escape—coffee shops, hidden corners of the library, quiet walks that felt like secrets just for them. Their love grew in those moments. But the shadow never fully lifted.

One afternoon, as they walked hand in hand between classes, Aimee felt her breath hitch. Harper appeared suddenly in their path. Her anxiety flared instantly. Aarav's grip tightened, instinctively pulling her closer as his gaze hardened.

"Harper," he said coldly. "What are you doing here?"

Reflection

Love can feel like safety—but real safety is tested when fear re-enters the room. Even as intimacy grows and bonds deepen, unresolved threats have a way of resurfacing. Healing doesn't happen in isolation from danger; it happens when connection stands firm in its presence.

Chapter 12

Harper looked different from the last time they had seen him. The arrogance that once defined him seemed stripped away, replaced by a weary, almost remorseful expression. His posture sagged, confidence dulled.

"Aarav. Aimee," he said quietly. "I've come to apologize."

Aimee stared at him, disbelief flickering across her face. "Apologize? For what?"

Harper took a slow breath, his gaze moving between them. "I was wrong. I let my pride and anger control me. I crossed lines I shouldn't have, and I'm here to make amends."

Skepticism rose quickly in Aimee's chest. The apology felt abrupt, uncharacteristic. "Why should we believe you?"

"I don't expect you to," Harper replied, meeting her eyes. "I can't undo what I did. I can only acknowledge it and try to do better."

Aimee glanced at Aarav. His stance relaxed slightly as he weighed Harper's words.

"If you're sincere," Aarav said finally, "we accept your apology. But trust isn't automatic. It has to be earned."

Harper nodded, relief briefly crossing his face. "I understand. I'll stay out of your way."

He turned and walked off, leaving them standing in silence—Aimee cautious, but willing to follow Aarav's lead.

The days that followed unfolded like a gentle reprieve. Aarav and Aimee leaned into their reconnection, allowing romance to bloom without restraint. Their hikes by the lake became ritual—quiet picnics beneath the trees, laughter echoing across the water, conversations filled with hopes and shared dreams. Intimacy deepened, emotionally and physically, as they spent nights talking beneath the stars, weaving tenderness into every moment.

Their differences still surfaced. Aarav's anxious attachment showed itself in his need for reassurance and closeness, while Aimee's avoidant tendencies nudged her toward solitude when emotions grew intense. Yet, instead of tearing them apart, these contrasts invited conversation. They learned, slowly, how to meet each other halfway.

One evening, stretched out on a blanket by the lake, Aarav rested his head on Aimee's shoulder.

"I'm glad we found our way back," he said softly. "It feels... right."

She ran her fingers through his hair, warmth spreading through her chest. "It does. Like things are finally settling."

As time passed, Harper faded into the background—no longer a looming threat, but a distant memory. Aimee's fear softened into cautious optimism, strengthened by the steadiness she felt with

Aarav. Their story became one of growth, of two people choosing to stay and evolve rather than retreat.

In the weeks after their heartfelt reconciliation, they embraced their relationship with renewed intention. Between lectures and late-night study sessions, their affection showed up in quiet ways—a hand held, a knowing smile, shared silence that felt safe. Still, as their bond strengthened, new complexities began to emerge.

Aimee found herself drawn toward something deeply personal. She joined the university's dance team, a decision fueled by passion and a desire for expression. Dancing became her refuge—a place where emotion transformed into movement. The studio, with its mirrored walls and polished wooden floors, quickly became a second home. She poured herself into rehearsals, staying late to perfect routines, her dedication unmistakable.

It was there she met Logan, one of the team's leads. He was magnetic—technically gifted, confident, and commanding attention the moment he stepped into the room. His energy filled the studio, and as rehearsals progressed, their partnership grew effortless, fluid, charged with creative chemistry that neither of them could ignore.

Reflection

Resolution doesn't mean the end of tension—it often marks the beginning of new tests. When connection deepens, growth invites unfamiliar dynamics that challenge security and self-awareness. Love doesn't ask us to stop evolving; it asks us to learn how to remain grounded while everything around us changes.

Chapter 13

Logan was of Mexican origin, strikingly handsome in a way that blended classic features with a rugged edge. His dark, wavy hair framed intense brown eyes that seemed to carry stories of their own. When he danced, he commanded the floor effortlessly—his movements a powerful mix of control and grace that drew every gaze toward him. Confidence followed him like a current, and when he stepped into a room, the energy shifted almost imperceptibly.

"Hey, Aimee," Logan greeted her one afternoon, his voice smooth and assured. "Ready to make some magic?"

Aimee smiled, anticipation flickering in her chest. "Absolutely. Let's get to work."

Their duet was a contemporary piece—fluid yet sharp, demanding both emotional depth and physical precision. As rehearsals unfolded, Aimee found herself swept into the intensity of Logan's presence. He pushed her beyond her limits, not with pressure, but with belief. Their time together was marked by laughter, discipline, and mutual respect, each movement strengthening their artistic connection. It was creative, focused, and deeply alive.

Despite the growing energy she shared with Logan on the dance floor, Aimee remained anchored in her commitment to Aarav. She was determined to nurture their relationship, even as dance began to claim more of her time and attention. Still, Aarav's anxious attachment surfaced quietly at first—through questions, silences, and the weight behind his concern.

One evening, after a long rehearsal, Aimee returned to her dorm to find Aarav waiting. His expression was tense, worry etched clearly across his face.

"Aimee, we need to talk," he said. "You've been spending so much time with Logan and the dance team. I'm starting to feel like I'm not a priority anymore."

She paused, choosing her words carefully. "Aarav, I'm still here. Dancing matters to me—it makes me happy. But that doesn't mean I care about you any less."

"It feels like you're slipping away," he admitted, frustration leaking through his voice. "I know it's my issue, but I can't shake the feeling that I'm losing you."

She reached for him, resting a steady hand on his arm. "I need you to trust me. I want to share this part of my life with you, not replace what we have."

The conversation ended without resolution, leaving both of them unsettled. Aarav's anxiety lingered, and Aimee's reassurance seemed only to deepen his fears. As they struggled to find balance between individuality and togetherness, small disruptions began to punctuate Aimee's days.

One afternoon, leaving the dance studio, she tripped over a loose tile and twisted her ankle. The injury was minor but painful, leaving her limping across campus. Aarav fussed with concern, but she brushed it off, insisting she was fine. Still, an uneasy feeling followed her—subtle, persistent.

Days later, she discovered her favorite dance shoes were missing. She searched everywhere—the studio, her dorm, every familiar corner—but they were nowhere to be found. Frustrated but undeterred, she borrowed a pair from another dancer and pushed forward.

Through it all, her dedication to dance never wavered. Rehearsals with Logan continued to energize her, their chemistry on stage sharpening with every practice. Their routines became seamless, a natural fusion of strength and expression. Logan's presence felt creatively invigorating, and Aimee found herself deeply fulfilled by the partnership they shared.

At the same time, Aarav's insecurity grew harder to ignore. Questions turned sharper, doubts more frequent. One night, after another long rehearsal, he confronted her again.

"Do you even realize how much time you spend with him?" Aarav said, frustration tightening his voice. "I see the way he looks at you, and it makes me uneasy."

Reflection

When growth pulls one partner outward, fear can pull the other inward. Passion and purpose aren't betrayals, but to an anxious heart, change can feel like abandonment. Love is tested not when attraction appears, but when trust must exist without constant reassurance.

Chapter 14

Aimee's patience was wearing thin.

"Logan and I are just dancing," she said firmly. "There's nothing more to it. I need you to trust me, Aarav."

"I do trust you," Aarav replied, his voice softening, though the tension in his shoulders remained. "But it's hard when I see you so absorbed in something—and someone—else."

The strain between them became impossible to ignore, a quiet pressure that followed every conversation. Aimee's avoidant tendencies made it difficult for her to stay present with Aarav's anxiety; when emotions intensified, her instinct was to retreat. Aarav, on the other hand, clung tighter, searching for reassurance that never seemed to fully land. Despite the friction, neither of them wanted to give up. They stayed—uncertain, imperfect, but committed to trying.

As days passed, the unsettling incidents around Aimee continued. She noticed fine scratches etched across her car's windshield one morning. Her phone glitched inexplicably, freezing and restarting at odd moments. She told herself it was coincidence, bad luck, nothing more—but a quiet unease settled in her chest, persistent and unresolved.

The tension finally reached a breaking point during a late-night conversation that stripped them both bare.

"I don't know if I can keep doing this," Aarav admitted, his voice shaking. "Every time I see you with Logan, every rehearsal, I feel like I'm losing you."

Aimee's heart clenched. "Aarav, I love you. I'm not leaving. But I'm trying to figure out who I am too—how to hold my passions without losing us."

"I need more from you," he said quietly. "And I don't know how to ask without pushing you away."

The honesty between them was raw and painful, illuminating what words had failed to soften before. Aarav's anxious attachment tightened his grip; Aimee's avoidant instinct urged distance. Neither was wrong—just wounded in different ways.

In the days that followed, their relationship oscillated between tenderness and tension. Some moments felt hopeful—shared laughter, gentle check-ins, familiar warmth. Others felt heavy, unresolved. Still, their bond endured, resilient in its refusal to break, even as it bent under pressure.

Meanwhile, Aimee's involvement with the dance team deepened. Dance remained her refuge and her release, even as it introduced new complications. Rehearsals with Logan grew increasingly demanding, their chemistry on the floor sharpening with every session. Logan was charismatic and commanding, his presence impossible to ignore. Each time he entered the studio, the energy shifted—confidence and intensity trailing him like a current.

"Ready to light up the floor today?" Logan asked one afternoon, his enthusiasm unmistakable.

Aimee nodded, grounding herself. "Absolutely. Let's make it unforgettable."

Their choreography required total synchronicity—precision, trust, emotional vulnerability expressed through movement. As they practiced, their connection translated effortlessly into the routine, passion and control weaving seamlessly together. Logan's praise came easily.

"You're really nailing this," he said with a grin. "I'm impressed by how quickly you've grown."

Aimee smiled, absorbing the validation—but beneath it all, she felt the growing weight of balance: between ambition and attachment, freedom and reassurance, expression and responsibility.

Reflection

When two attachment wounds collide, love can begin to feel like pressure instead of safety. Anxious hearts seek closeness to soothe fear; avoidant hearts seek distance to stay regulated. Healing doesn't come from choosing one over the other—it comes from learning how to stay present when both are uncomfortable.

Chapter 15

Aimee's cheeks flushed with genuine pleasure. "Thank you," she said warmly. "I'm really enjoying working with you."

The connection between them was undeniable—rooted in mutual respect, discipline, and a shared creative purpose. Their partnership thrived within the boundaries of dance, yet outside the studio, Aarav's anxiety continued to simmer, quietly seeping into moments that were meant to feel joyful.

One evening, after a particularly grueling rehearsal, Aarav waited outside the studio. When Aimee finally stepped out, still catching her breath, he approached her—his expression a blend of concern and frustration.

"You were incredible tonight," he said, though there was an edge beneath the compliment. "But you're late. I've been waiting for hours."

"I'm sorry," Aimee replied, her smile fading. "I lost track of time. The routine is demanding, and I wanted to get it right."

"I get that," Aarav said quietly. "It just feels like I'm always the one waiting. I need to know I still matter."

"You do," she said softly. "But this matters to me too. I need you to trust that I'm not pushing you away."

The conversation ended without resolution, leaving both unsettled. Aarav's anxiety tightened its grip, while Aimee's instinct was to pull inward, unsure how to soothe fears she didn't fully understand how to carry.

As the days passed, the unsettling incidents escalated. One morning, Aimee discovered her car tires slashed, leaving her stranded and shaken. Though a friend helped her get to campus, the unease lingered. It no longer felt random. The shadow of Harper—never fully confronted—crept back into her thoughts.

Still, Aimee poured herself into dance. Rehearsals became her refuge, the rhythm of movement offering clarity when everything else felt fractured. Logan remained a steady presence—focused, encouraging, and creatively aligned. Dancing with him felt grounding, purposeful.

One evening, after an especially intense rehearsal, Aimee and Logan sat on the studio floor, catching their breath. The usual buzz of the room had faded, leaving a rare stillness.

"You know," Logan said thoughtfully, "I really enjoy dancing with you. There's something special about how we connect."

Aimee smiled, calm settling over her. "I feel it too. It's like we're in sync—emotionally and physically."

"I'm glad we're partners," he said gently. "It's been a great experience."

Meanwhile, Aarav's doubts grew heavier. Questions turned into arguments. One night, exhausted and overwhelmed, he finally broke.

"I'm tired of this, Aimee," he said, voice rising. "Every time I see you with Logan, it feels like I'm losing you."

"I've told you," she replied, frustration edging in. "He's just my dance partner. My feelings for you haven't changed. But I need you to trust me."

"I want to," Aarav said, voice shaking. "But I feel like I'm always on the outside."

Their conversations began to circle the same wounds, leaving them both drained. Aarav clung harder; Aimee struggled to stay emotionally present without feeling overwhelmed. Still, she tried—balancing rehearsals with intentional time together, even as the unexplained incidents added tension to her days.

One afternoon, practicing alone in the studio, Aimee paused mid-movement. A strange sensation prickled at the back of her neck—the unmistakable feeling of being watched. She scanned the mirrors, the corners, the doorway. The studio was empty. The feeling passed, but unease lingered. She shook it off and kept dancing, refusing to let fear steal yet another piece of herself.

Reflection

When reassurance becomes a demand and independence feels like abandonment, love begins to strain under expectations it was never meant to carry. Unresolved fear doesn't always announce itself loudly—sometimes it shows up as control, suspicion, or silence. True safety is built not through constant proximity, but through trust that holds even when paths momentarily diverge.

Chapter 16

As the week unfolded, Aarav and Aimee's relationship became a delicate dance of its own. They struggled to balance individual passions with shared intimacy, their conversations swinging between heartfelt confessions and exhausting misunderstandings. Still, beneath the friction, love remained—a steady undercurrent that neither was ready to abandon.

Their quiet moments offered relief. Soft conversations late at night, gentle touches, familiar warmth—these were reminders of what bound them together. Yet tension lingered, unspoken but ever-present, shaped by their opposing attachment needs. Love brought them close; fear kept pulling them apart.

As the weekend approached, they decided to escape campus for a while. A hike to a scenic overlook promised space, clarity, and a chance to reconnect without distractions. The trail wound through dense forest, sunlight filtering through the canopy above. They walked hand in hand, the stillness of nature easing the weight they had been carrying.

At the overlook, the valley stretched endlessly below them. They sat on a sun-warmed rock, backs resting against each other, sharing a comfortable silence that felt earned.

"I'm glad we did this," Aarav said quietly. "It feels good to step away for a bit."

Aimee smiled, her chest lightening. "Me too. Moments like this remind me why I fell in love with you."

They talked—about dreams, fears, hopes they rarely voiced aloud. The hike softened something between them, grounding their connection in shared presence rather than constant reassurance. As the sun dipped lower, bathing the landscape in gold, they began their walk back, renewed but not fully healed.

Back on campus, the unease returned. The strange incidents continued to hover unresolved—scratches, missing items, that persistent sense of being watched. Aimee pushed the worry aside, focusing instead on Aarav and dance, determined not to let fear dictate her life.

But the weeks that followed brought mounting strain. Aarav's anxiety intensified, and each interaction seemed to amplify their differences. Conversations that began calmly often spiraled into conflict.

One afternoon, as Aimee left rehearsal, Aarav stopped her in the hallway, tension etched into his face.

"Aimee, we need to talk."

She exhaled sharply. "Not again, Aarav. Can we please just have one peaceful day?"

"I'm tired of feeling second place," he said, voice rising. "You spend so much time with Logan. I feel like I'm losing you."

"Logan is just my dance partner," she replied tightly.

"Then why does it feel like I'm always competing for your attention?" His desperation cracked through. "I need to know where I stand."

Aimee's frustration spilled over.

"I love you," she said firmly. "But this constant insecurity is suffocating me. I need space—to breathe, to be myself."

The argument ended without resolution. Distance settled in its wake. Aarav's clinginess—born from fear, not malice—had become a weight Aimee no longer knew how to carry. And for the first time, she began to wonder if love alone was enough to survive the pressure building between them.

Reflection

Love doesn't fail because two people care too little—it falters when fear speaks louder than trust. When reassurance becomes a demand and space feels like rejection, intimacy turns into tension. Sometimes the hardest question isn't do we love each other? but can we grow without losing ourselves in the process?

Chapter 17

Meanwhile, Aimee's rehearsals with Logan grew more intense. Logan's charm was undeniable—sharp wit paired with an ease that filled the studio. His confidence flirted with arrogance, and he had a way of both encouraging and irritating her in equal measure, pushing her limits while quietly drawing her in.

"You know," Logan teased one afternoon, a mischievous grin playing on his lips, "you make this routine look effortless. It's like you were born to dance."

Aimee rolled her eyes, though a smile betrayed her. "Flattery will get you everywhere, Logan."

Their sessions became a whirlwind of energy. Logan danced boldly, commanding space with sharp, dynamic movements. He complimented her often—sometimes sincerely, sometimes tinged with self-satisfaction.

"You're really bringing your A-game today," he said once. "Almost makes me think you're trying to outshine me."

Aimee laughed. "Hardly. I just want us to nail the performance."

Though his attention was flattering, it stirred an undercurrent of unease. She enjoyed the partnership, valued the creative chemistry, but remained deliberate in keeping their connection strictly professional. That boundary mattered—to her, and to the person waiting beyond the studio walls.

As competition day approached, the atmosphere inside the studio crackled with anticipation. The team buzzed with nervous excitement, and Logan and Aimee's duo was whispered about as the highlight of the night. Rehearsals sharpened, intensity rising with every run-through.

The auditorium filled quickly on the day of the performance, excitement humming through the air. Aarav arrived early, settling into his seat with a tight knot in his chest. He reminded himself—I'm here to support her. He cheered politely for the early acts, forcing his focus forward, steadying his breath.

When Logan and Aimee finally stepped onto the stage, the room fell silent. From the first beat of music, they commanded attention. Their choreography blended precision with sensual fluidity, every movement intentional. Logan thrived under the spotlight, his confidence unmistakable. Aimee matched him step for step, grounded and luminous.

They moved in perfect synchronization—spins, lifts, and moments of closeness woven seamlessly together. When Logan executed a daring lift, the audience gasped. His eyes never left Aimee as he guided her through the motion, admiration plain. The chemistry between them pulsed outward, unmistakable.

The routine built toward a breathtaking finale, ending in a sequence that brought the audience to its feet. Applause thundered through the hall as they took their bows, the standing ovation sealing the performance's impact.

Aarav watched, heart pounding. Pride warred with something darker as he absorbed the murmurs around him.

"Did you see how they moved together?" someone whispered. "It's like they were made for each other."

"I've never seen chemistry like that," another voice chimed in.

Aarav's hands clenched. Each comment landed like a quiet blow. He tried to focus on Aimee's radiant smile as she bowed, to hold onto the truth of what they shared—but jealousy and fear crept in, relentless, overwhelming his resolve.

Reflection

When admiration turns public, insecurity often turns private—and louder. Anxious attachment doesn't fear attraction itself; it fears replacement. In moments like these, the real battle isn't between rivals on a stage, but between trust and the stories fear insists on telling.

Chapter 18

When the performance ended, Aimee and Logan received their well-earned accolades. The applause still rang in her ears as she held the trophy, pride glowing through her exhaustion. Yet as her eyes searched the crowd instinctively, her smile faltered. Aarav wasn't there.

A quiet unease settled in her chest. She scanned the auditorium again—rows of faces, flashes of excitement, whispered praise—but no sign of him. Her joy dimmed, replaced by a growing knot of worry. Excusing herself, she hurried backstage, weaving through corridors and dressing rooms, dialing his number again and again. Each call went unanswered.

"Aarav... where are you?" Her voice trembled as she moved through the empty halls. "Please. Come back."

The silence pressed in on her. With every unanswered ring, panic crept closer to the surface. Eventually, she found herself back in the now-quiet auditorium, trophy clutched tightly against her chest, its weight suddenly unbearable. What should have been one of the happiest nights of her life felt hollow without him.

Hours passed in a blur. Messages went unread. Calls unanswered. Celebration turned into dread. When she finally returned to her dorm, moonlight spilled through the window as she sat on her bed, phone resting uselessly beside her. Fear tangled with frustration, guilt threading through it all. Aarav's disappearance felt like a rupture—one that echoed every unresolved argument, every unspoken fear.

By dawn, hope had thinned to something fragile. She knew they were standing at the edge of something irreversible, and the past days had pushed them there faster than she could comprehend.

The following day was heavy with uncertainty. Aimee searched relentlessly—his dorm, the library, cafés they once frequented. She asked friends, retraced familiar paths, lingered in places that still carried his presence. Everywhere she went, silence answered her.

Fear deepened. The strange incidents that had followed her for weeks—scratches, missing items, that sense of being watched—returned to her thoughts, now sharper, more menacing. Unable to bear the uncertainty any longer, she filed a missing person's report. The police issued an alert. Word spread quickly across campus. Unease settled over the university like a low, gathering storm.

Later that day, Aimee sat at a canteen bench, barely able to swallow a bite of food as friends surrounded her, offering comfort she could hardly absorb. Then she saw him.

Harper.

He walked past with his group, still powerful, still untouchable. As he glanced at her, a slow, devious grin spread across his face before he turned away. Aimee's heart began to race. The fear that gripped her chest felt sharper now—more focused.

The days that followed were some of the hardest she had ever endured. Her thoughts spiraled endlessly—confusion, terror, guilt all colliding without relief. Every corner of the campus carried memories of Aarav: laughter between classes, quiet moments, promises whispered too soon. Her phone never left her hand, the absence of replies a constant ache.

She searched everywhere—again and again. His dorm. The library. The café where they used to sit between lectures. Their favorite quiet spots, where she half-expected to find him waiting, smiling like nothing had gone wrong.

But he was nowhere.

Reflection

When an anxious heart disappears, it doesn't vanish quietly—it leaves echoes behind. Silence becomes its own form of pain, forcing unanswered questions to grow louder with every passing hour. In moments like these, fear no longer whispers; it takes shape, demanding to be faced, whether we are ready or not.

Chapter 19

Days slipped into a week, and still there was no sign of Aarav. It was as if he had vanished without a trace. No sightings. No messages. Nothing. With each passing day, the hope Aimee clung to began to thin, fraying at the edges.

She tried to return to routine—classes, rehearsals, deadlines—but her heart wasn't in any of it. The dance studio, once her sanctuary, now felt suffocating. The mirrors reflected exhaustion instead of passion. Logan and the upcoming competition demanded focus, but all Aimee could see when she closed her eyes was Aarav—his face tight with emotion, the way he had looked at her before walking out of the auditorium that night.

Logan noticed. He always did.

One afternoon, he leaned against the mirrored wall, arms crossed, watching her move through the choreography without conviction.

"You're distracted," he said plainly. "What's going on?"

Aimee wiped sweat from her forehead, avoiding his reflection. "It's nothing. I'm fine."

Logan raised an eyebrow. "You've been off all week. If this is about Aarav—"

"It's not," she cut in, though her voice cracked under the lie.

He sighed, stepping closer, his tone gentler. "Whatever's happening between you two—you can't let it take over your head. We've got a competition coming up."

Her composure finally broke. "He's missing, Logan," she said quietly. "No one's seen him for over a week. I'm scared something's happened to him."

Logan's expression shifted instantly. "Missing? You're serious?"

She nodded, tears burning. "I don't know where he is. And I don't know what to do."

He hesitated, then placed a steady hand on her shoulder. "We'll figure it out. But you have to take care of yourself first. You won't help him if you fall apart."

She appreciated his concern, but it didn't quiet the anxiety tightening in her chest. As the days stretched on in silence, Aimee felt herself unraveling—slowly, painfully.

One night, after another unanswered call, she lay on her bed staring at the ceiling, replaying every word of their last conversation. Had she missed something? Ignored a warning? Why would Aarav disappear like this—without a word, without goodbye?

Her phone buzzed on the nightstand.

Her breath caught as she lunged for it, hope surging—

—and then collapsing.

It wasn't Aarav.

It was Harper.

Aimee stared at the screen, her thumb hovering uncertainly. She hadn't heard from him since the night in the jungle, since his apology. She didn't trust him. Something about him still set her nerves on edge.

And yet, a sick certainty settled in her gut.

Harper might know something about Aarav's disappearance.

Reflection

When someone vanishes without closure, the mind searches relentlessly for meaning. Anxious attachment doesn't just fear loss—it fears unanswered absence. Silence becomes a breeding ground for dread, and the past is replayed not for nostalgia, but for clues we hope will explain the unexplainable.

Chapter 20

With a steadying breath, Aimee answered the call.

"Hello?"

"Aimee." Harper's voice slid through the line—smooth, controlled. "We need to talk."

Her grip tightened around the phone. "I don't have anything to say to you, Harper."

"I think you'll want to hear what I have to say," he replied calmly. "It's about Aarav."

Her heart skipped painfully. "What do you know?"

"Meet me at the old library tomorrow night," Harper said, sidestepping her question. "We'll talk then."

Before she could protest, the line went dead.

Aimee stared at the phone, dread and resolve settling into her bones. She didn't trust Harper—not for a second. But if he knew anything about Aarav, she couldn't afford to ignore him. She would go. And she would be ready.

The next night, she approached the old library, her pulse loud in her ears. The building stood forgotten at the edge of campus, its once-grand façade dulled by time. She pushed open the heavy wooden doors and stepped inside. Dust clung to the air. Dim light stretched long shadows across rows of abandoned shelves.

Harper waited in the center of the room, leaning casually against a desk. When he saw her, a smug smile tugged at his mouth.

"I knew you'd come," he said, satisfaction lacing his voice.

Aimee folded her arms, keeping her distance. "What do you know about Aarav?"

His smile widened. "He's in trouble, Aimee. Big trouble."

Her stomach dropped. "What kind of trouble?"

Harper stepped closer, his eyes glinting in a way that made her skin crawl. "Let's just say he crossed people he shouldn't have. And now, he's paying for it."

Her thoughts raced. "What do you mean? Who did this?"

For the briefest moment, his confidence faltered. Uncertainty flickered behind his eyes. "I can't give you everything," he said carefully. "But Aarav's disappearance wasn't an accident."

Anger surged through her. "Did you have something to do with this?"

Harper lifted his hands in mock surrender. "Me? No. But I know the ones who did."

Her chest tightened. "Where is he, Harper?" she demanded. "Tell me where he is."

Reflection

When fear meets desperation, even the untrustworthy begin to look like answers. In moments of crisis, boundaries blur and instincts sharpen—not because trust has grown, but because love refuses to stay still in the face of uncertainty. Sometimes courage isn't knowing who to believe; it's choosing to step forward anyway.

Chapter 21

Harper's eyes darkened. "He's in a place you won't be able to reach," he said quietly. "But I might be able to help you... for a price."

Aimee's hands curled into fists. "What do you want?"

He stepped closer, lowering his voice to a dangerous whisper. "I want you to stop dancing with Logan."

She stared at him. "What?"

"You heard me," Harper said coldly. "Quit the dance team. Cut Logan out of your life. Do that—and I'll tell you where Aarav is."

Her thoughts spun violently. The demand was absurd, cruel—but the stakes were unbearable. Aarav's life hung in the balance, and pride, passion, even identity felt suddenly insignificant.

"Fine," she said through clenched teeth. "I'll quit. Now tell me where he is."

Harper smiled, devoid of warmth. "I'll be in touch."

He left her standing alone in the library, fear and rage crashing through her chest in equal measure.

The days that followed blurred into numbness. Aimee stepped away from the dance team without explanation, her absence rippling through rehearsals. Logan was stunned, then hurt.

"You're just quitting?" he demanded. "After everything we built?"

"I don't have a choice," she said hollowly.

"There's always a choice," he snapped. "You're just afraid to make the right one."

She didn't argue. She didn't have the strength. Every thought, every breath, was consumed by Aarav.

Days passed. Harper stayed silent. Her anxiety grew unbearable.

Then, one evening, a message arrived from an unknown number.

Meet me at the docks tonight. Come alone.

Her heart pounded. She knew it was Harper. She also knew this was her only chance.

The docks were cold and quiet, water lapping against the wood under a moonless sky. Harper stood in the shadows, barely visible.

"Where is he?" Aimee demanded, voice shaking.

"He's closer than you think," Harper replied darkly.

A sound behind her made her turn—and her breath left her body.

Aarav.

Bruised. Bloodied. Chained to a metal post near the water's edge.

"Aarav!" she screamed, rushing forward.

Harper yanked her back. "Not so fast."

"Let him go!" she cried, fighting his grip.

"Not until you keep your promise," Harper snarled. "You're done dancing. For good."

The truth hit her all at once. This wasn't power. This was obsession. Control disguised as leverage.

Anger surged, burning away fear.

In a sudden burst of strength, Aimee wrenched herself free and ran to Aarav. Her hands shook as she worked at the chains, fingers slick with panic and urgency.

"You'll regret this," Harper shouted behind her.

But Aimee didn't look back.

All she could see was Aarav.

All she could think was get him free.

Reflection

Control often wears the mask of sacrifice—asking you to give up who you are in exchange for someone you love. But love that demands erasure is not love; it is captivity. In moments like this, courage isn't choosing the lesser loss—it's refusing to believe that saving someone requires losing yourself.

Chapter 22

Ignoring him, Aimee kept working at the chains with trembling hands until, at last, they fell away with a dull metallic clatter. Aarav collapsed forward, weak and shaking, and she caught him instinctively, holding him as if letting go might make him disappear again.

Tears streamed down her face as she pressed her forehead to his. "I'm so sorry, Aarav. I should've been there for you."

His voice was hoarse, barely more than a whisper. "It's not your fault, Aimee. I'm just... glad you found me."

Together, unsteady and exhausted, they moved away from the docks, leaving Harper behind in the darkness.

The nightmare wasn't over—not really—but Aimee knew one thing with absolute certainty: she would never allow anyone to come between them again. They made a conscious decision not to tell the university or the authorities. Neither of them wanted more chaos, more questions, more fear. But inside herself, Aimee made a quiet promise—this will never happen again. No matter the cost.

The weeks following Aarav's rescue were heavy with a strange mix of relief and tension. Life slowly returned to something resembling normal, but it felt altered, as though the world had tilted slightly off its axis. Aarav tried to push past the trauma, forcing himself into routines, pretending strength where he still felt fractured. With Aimee by his side, he functioned—but healing was uneven.

Their bond had deepened, but it had also grown more complicated. Aarav's anxiety intensified; he checked in constantly, needed reassurance more often, as though losing her once had rewired something inside him. Aimee noticed it all. And though she still cared deeply, something within her had shifted too. The danger had drained her emotionally, leaving her reflective, distant at times. Thoughts of the future crept in—of cultural differences, of expectations, of what it truly meant to love someone whose fears could so easily become her responsibility.

That was when Tia entered their lives.

One bright afternoon, Aimee and Aarav lay on the grass outside the university, the warmth of the sun soothing after a long day of classes. Aarav seemed lighter than he had in weeks, his fingers loosely intertwined with hers, his breathing calm. Just as Aimee allowed herself to relax, his phone buzzed.

He glanced at the screen and sat up abruptly.

"What is it?" Aimee asked, sensing the shift.

Aarav smiled, though a trace of nervous energy crept into his expression. "It's Tia. She's here."

"Your sister?" Aimee asked.

"Yeah," he said, running a hand through his hair. "She's visiting from India. She didn't tell me she was coming—but she's in New York."

His phone buzzed again, and he answered. "Tia! What are you doing here?"

Aimee listened quietly as he spoke, his tone affectionate and familiar. She had heard about Tia often—independent, sharp, deeply bonded to Aarav. Still, the suddenness of the visit unsettled her. The timing felt... significant.

When Aarav ended the call, he turned to her. "She's staying near campus. I'm meeting her for dinner. Would you like to come?"

Aimee hesitated. Meeting his family—really meeting them—felt like crossing an invisible threshold. Questions flooded her mind. Would Tia like her? Would she approve? Would she see what Aimee herself was still trying to understand?

Then she saw the hope in Aarav's eyes.

"Sure," she said softly. "I'd love to."

That evening, they met Tia at a small, cozy restaurant not far from campus. The moment Aimee saw her, she understood why Aarav spoke of her with such affection. Tia was striking—long dark hair, sharp features, and an effortless confidence that filled the room. She carried herself with ease, the kind of presence that didn't need permission to be noticed.

"Tia," Aarav said warmly, "this is Aimee."

Tia looked at her, smiling—curious, assessing, unmistakably attentive.

Reflection

Survival can bind people tightly, but it can also quietly change them. Trauma doesn't always break love—it reshapes it. What once felt simple becomes layered with fear, vigilance, and unspoken questions about the future. Healing isn't just about staying together; it's about noticing who you become afterward—and deciding whether love still allows space for both people to breathe.

Chapter 23

Aimee extended her hand, suddenly aware of herself under Tia's steady, assessing gaze. "It's really nice to meet you," she said, forcing a calm she didn't entirely feel.

Tia smiled and shook her hand, her grip firm, her expression warm but measured. "Nice to meet you too, Aimee. I've heard a lot about you."

Aimee wondered—what kind of a lot? She glanced at Aarav, who was smiling broadly, clearly thrilled to have his sister there. Yet beneath the pleasant exchange, Aimee sensed something faint but unmistakable: tension. Tia was kind, polite—but there was a formality to her warmth, as if she were keeping a careful distance.

As they sat down for dinner, conversation flowed easily at first. Tia asked about Aimee's studies, her interests, her plans after graduation. She listened attentively, nodding at the right moments, smiling when appropriate. Still, as the evening unfolded, Aimee began to feel as though each question carried a quiet evaluation—subtle, unspoken, but present.

"So, Aimee," Tia said casually, her eyes sharp despite her relaxed tone, "how are you finding New York? It must be very different from where you grew up."

Aimee nodded. "It is different—but I love it here. It's been a really meaningful experience for me."

Tia smiled, though something unreadable flickered across her face. "And how do you find the culture here compared to ours? Do you think you'd ever want to visit India?"

The question caught Aimee off guard. She glanced at Aarav, who was busy pouring water into their glasses, unaware of the subtle shift in the conversation.

"I'd love to visit someday," Aimee replied carefully. "Aarav's told me so much about it."

Tia's smile widened, but it didn't quite reach her eyes. "India is... very different. Our family has certain expectations—especially when it comes to relationships. Things are more traditional."

The words landed softly, but their weight was unmistakable. Aimee felt a tightness form in her chest. There it was—the invisible line she had always sensed but never fully confronted. The cultural divide she had tried not to dwell on was now standing plainly between them.

Aarav finally looked up, blissfully unaware. "Tia, I thought we could show you around campus tomorrow. Maybe grab lunch too. Aimee can come with us."

Tia's expression softened. "That sounds nice."

The next day unfolded pleasantly on the surface. They wandered through campus, stopped at local cafés, even took a short hike nearby. Laughter came easily. Yet for Aimee, the unease never fully lifted. Tia was courteous, even warm—but always just distant enough to feel unreachable, as though she were silently measuring Aimee against a standard no one had explained.

And slowly, doubt crept in.

Aimee found herself thinking more about Aarav's family, about the world he came from. Stories he had once shared lightly—about traditions, responsibilities, and family honor—now carried a different gravity. She had always known their backgrounds were different. But now, those differences felt heavier, sharper, harder to ignore.

One afternoon, seated in a quiet café, Tia returned to the subject with deliberate calm.

"So, Aimee," she said, stirring her coffee, "what are your plans for the future? Do you see yourself settling down here in the U.S.?"

Aimee hesitated. "I'm not sure. I think it depends on where life takes me."

Tia nodded slowly. "Aarav will eventually go back to India. Our parents expect him to take over the family business. It's not something he can simply walk away from."

Aimee's gaze flicked to Aarav, who was distracted by his phone, unaware that a quiet truth was being laid bare beside him. Her heart sank. She had known his family was influential—but she hadn't realized how predetermined his future might be.

"I didn't know that," she said softly, the words barely audible.

Reflection

Sometimes, love doesn't fracture because of conflict—but because of unspoken futures. Cultural expectations, family loyalty, and inherited paths can quietly overshadow even the strongest connection. When love meets a life already mapped out, the question isn't just do we love each other—it becomes do our worlds allow us to choose each other freely?

Chapter 24

Tia's smile softened, almost sympathetic. "It's a big responsibility," she said gently. "Our family is very traditional, and there are certain... expectations when it comes to who Aarav will marry. My parents are very particular about these things."

Aimee felt her heart pound as the words settled in. She had always sensed that their relationship would face resistance, but hearing it stated so plainly made it feel unavoidable—almost predetermined. What once felt like distant possibilities now stood right in front of her, solid and unyielding.

After that conversation, Aimee couldn't shake the feeling that she was intruding on a life that wasn't meant to fully include her. No matter how deeply she and Aarav loved each other, there seemed to be an entire world—his family, his future, his obligations—that she could never truly belong to. The cultural differences she had once brushed aside now loomed large, casting a quiet shadow over every shared moment.

Over the next few days, her doubts deepened. Without fully realizing it, Aimee began to pull away. She avoided Aarav's touch, sidestepped his attempts at affection, and found reasons to keep herself busy when he wanted to spend time together.

Aarav noticed immediately.

"Aimee, what's going on?" he asked one evening as they sat in her dorm room. His voice was careful but strained, his eyes searching her face.

She shook her head, forcing a small smile. "Nothing, Aarav. I'm just tired."

But he didn't let it go. His anxiety, already simmering, surged forward. He reached for her hand, gripping it tightly. "You've been distant. I can feel it. Is this because of Tia? Did she say something to you?"

Aimee hesitated. She didn't want to hurt him—but the weight inside her chest was too heavy to carry alone. "She didn't say anything directly," she said quietly. "But... Aarav, I don't know if this is going to work. We come from such different worlds. Your family—they'll never accept me."

His face fell, and his grip tightened. "Don't say that," he pleaded. "I don't care what my family thinks. I love you. That's what matters."

"But does it?" Aimee whispered, her voice trembling. "What happens when you have to go back to India? When your parents expect you to marry someone from your culture—someone they choose?"

Panic flickered across Aarav's face. "I'll figure it out," he said desperately. "We'll figure it out together. Please don't pull away from me. I can't lose you."

Her heart ached at the fear in his voice. But the doubts refused to quiet. She had seen the subtle judgment in Tia's eyes, heard the warning beneath her careful words. And deep down, Aimee knew—this wasn't just insecurity. It was reality.

A few days later, the truth finally surfaced.

Aimee and Tia went for a walk together, hoping—at least on Aimee's part—to bridge the growing distance between them. Their conversation was light at first, but suddenly Tia stopped, turning to face her with an expression far more serious than before.

"Aimee, there's something I need to tell you," she said softly. "My father sent me here."

Aimee frowned. "What do you mean?"

Tia exhaled slowly. "He wanted me to check on Aarav. He's worried about him—about the choices he's making. Especially when it comes to you."

Aimee felt the ground shift beneath her. "Your father doesn't approve of me," she said quietly.

Tia shook her head. "It's not personal. It's just... our family has expectations. My father believes this relationship is distracting Aarav from his responsibilities. He doesn't think you're the right fit for his future."

The words landed like a slow, sinking weight. Aimee felt nauseous—not from surprise, but from confirmation. She had known this was coming. She had felt it in every guarded glance, every carefully worded question.

"I'm sorry," Tia added, her voice gentle. "But I thought you deserved to know."

Reflection

Sometimes, the most painful truths aren't spoken in anger—but in quiet certainty. When love collides with inherited expectations, the struggle isn't about effort or devotion—it's about belonging. And realizing that you may never fit into someone else's future can be more heartbreaking than losing them outright.

Chapter 25

Aimee nodded, her thoughts spiraling faster than she could steady them. She had always known that loving Aarav wouldn't be simple—but now it felt overwhelming, almost impossible. How could she stay with him knowing his family didn't approve? How could she ever ask him to choose between her and the life that had already been mapped out for him long before she existed?

As they walked back toward campus, a quiet heaviness settled inside her. She loved Aarav deeply—but for the first time, she began to question whether love alone could withstand the weight of tradition, expectation, and future obligations.

In the days that followed, Aimee pulled back without fully meaning to. Aarav, sensing the distance, responded in the only way he knew how—by holding on tighter. He called constantly, sent message after message, showed up unannounced at her dorm, searching her face for reassurance that she was still there, that she hadn't already left him in her heart.

But the more he clung, the more suffocated Aimee felt. His anxiety pressed in on her, mixing with her own doubts until it became unbearable.

One evening, after yet another argument that left them both raw and exhausted, Aimee finally broke.

"Aarav, I can't do this anymore," she said, her voice cracking. "I feel like I'm drowning."

His face drained of color. His hands trembled as he reached for her. "Please don't say that," he begged. "We can work through this. I'll do anything—just don't leave me."

Tears streamed down her face as she shook her head. "I love you, Aarav. I really do. But I don't know if love is enough. Your family doesn't accept me, and I can't keep pretending that it doesn't matter. I don't want to come between you and them."

The words shattered something inside him. Panic surged, sharp and uncontrollable. "You are everything to me," he said desperately. "I don't care what my family thinks. I'll choose you. Always."

But Aimee could see it—the fear in his eyes, the way his world seemed to collapse around the possibility of losing her. And she knew this wasn't love anymore. It was survival.

"I need time," she whispered. "I need to figure out what I want."

Aarav stood frozen as she walked away, his chest aching with a pain he had never known. Every instinct screamed at him to chase her, to beg, to hold on—but for the first time, he didn't.

For the first time, Aarav let her go.

That evening, Aarav sat across from Tia at the dinner table, the silence between them heavy and oppressive. His plate remained untouched, the food growing cold as his thoughts spiraled. Tia watched him carefully, sensing the storm beneath his stillness.

Finally, he spoke.

"Tia... I don't understand," he said, his voice low and strained. "Why does Aimee want to walk away from me? I've tried so hard. You've seen it. I've done everything to make her feel loved. Why would she say that love isn't enough?"

Tia looked down at her hands, guilt tightening in her chest. She hadn't anticipated this—hadn't imagined the depth of her brother's pain. Seeing Aarav like this, unraveling, filled her with a quiet shame.

"It's not that you didn't love her enough," she said gently, though her voice wavered. "Maybe she's just overwhelmed. With everything going on... maybe she's scared."

Aarav stared into his drink, his grip tightening until his knuckles turned white. "Scared of what?" he asked, frustration breaking through. "I've tried to make everything perfect. I've shown her that she's my future. Why does she think this won't work? Why does she keep bringing up my family like it's an impossible obstacle?"

The question lingered between them—heavy, unanswered, and painfully honest.

Reflection

When anxious love meets emotional withdrawal, both people suffer in different ways. One clings out of fear of abandonment; the other retreats to breathe. Neither is wrong—but without awareness, love turns into pressure, and connection turns into pain. Sometimes, letting go isn't giving up—it's the first act of self-respect for both hearts involved.

Chapter 26

Tia's breath caught in her throat. She bit down on her lip, fighting the urge to blurt out the truth right then. She had wanted to protect Aarav—shield him from pain—but with every word he spoke, the guilt pressed harder against her chest, almost unbearable now.

Aarav looked up at her, his eyes raw and searching.

"Tia, you've spent time with Aimee. You've seen us together," he said quietly. "Do you think... do you think there's something wrong with me? Am I too much for her? Or is it my family? Is there something I'm not seeing?"

The question shattered whatever resolve Tia had left.

"I don't know what to think anymore," Aarav continued, his voice strained. "I love her so much. I can't lose her. But I don't know how to make her believe in us again. She's slipping away, and it feels like there's nothing I can do."

Tia turned her face away, tears blurring her vision. The weight of her silence had become unbearable. If she didn't speak now, she knew she never would.

"Aarav..." she whispered.

He looked up instantly, startled by the tremor in her voice. "What is it? What's wrong?"

Her chest tightened as the truth finally broke free.

"It's not you," she said, tears spilling over. "It's not you at all. It's... it's our family. It's Dad."

Aarav froze.

"What do you mean?" he asked, barely audible.

Tia's voice cracked as she forced the words out.

"Dad sent me here. He wanted me to watch you. To see how things were going between you and Aimee. He didn't approve of her—from the beginning."

Aarav felt the air leave his lungs.

"What?" he whispered.

"I didn't want to do it," Tia sobbed. "I swear. But Dad pressured me. He said you weren't thinking clearly. That you were letting emotions cloud your judgment. He thinks Aimee will pull you away—from the family, from India, from everything he's built. He wanted me to talk to her... to understand her intentions. And if needed—discourage her."

The realization hit Aarav like a blow to the chest.

All this time, he had been fighting himself—his anxiety, his fear of abandonment—while his own family had been quietly working against him.

"You're telling me," he said slowly, disbelief sharpening his tone, "that Dad sent you here to sabotage my relationship? To monitor me like I'm a child who can't make his own choices?"

Tia wiped her tears, shame etched into every movement.

"He thought he was protecting you. He wants you to marry someone from India. Someone who fits. Someone who understands our traditions."

Aarav stood abruptly, pacing the room, anger burning through his veins.

"And you went along with it?" he snapped. "You lied to me. You watched me fall apart. Do you have any idea what you've done? Aimee is pulling away because of this—because of you. Because you planted doubts she was already struggling with."

"I didn't mean to hurt you," Tia cried. "I didn't know how to say no to him. He kept calling, asking for updates. I didn't know how to tell him you were serious."

Aarav slammed his hand against the table, the sharp clatter of cutlery breaking the silence.

"You should have told him to back off!" he shouted. "You should have told him this is my life. That I get to choose who I love!"

His voice cracked as the rage gave way to something far more painful. Betrayal. Loss. Grief.

He turned away from her, chest heaving—not just from anger, but from the devastating realization that the distance between him and Aimee hadn't been accidental at all.

Reflection

Sometimes the deepest wounds don't come from lovers—they come from loyalty misplaced. When family control disguises itself as concern, it quietly erodes autonomy, trust, and love. And when truth arrives too late, it doesn't just explain the distance—it reveals who unknowingly helped create it.

Chapter 27

Tia flinched at his outburst, tears streaming freely down her face.

"Aarav, I'm so sorry," she whispered. "I never wanted this to happen. I never wanted to come between you and Aimee. I didn't realize how much she meant to you until I saw you together. I thought maybe... maybe it was just a phase."

Aarav let out a hollow, bitter laugh, his back still turned to her.

"A phase?" he repeated quietly. "You thought my love for Aimee was a phase?"

He shook his head, disbelief and rage tangled in his voice. "You and Dad have no idea how much she means to me. She's not a fling, Tia. She's my future. She's the one person who made me feel like I finally belonged somewhere. And now she's slipping away—because Dad can't stop controlling every part of my life."

Tia's sobs softened, but she remained frozen, paralyzed by regret.

"I thought I was doing what was best for you," she said weakly.

Aarav turned to face her at last. His eyes burned—not just with anger, but with heartbreak.

"You thought tearing apart the only thing that's ever made me happy was what's best for me?" he asked. "You thought betraying me like this was love?"

Tia lowered her gaze.

"I was wrong," she said quietly. "I see that now."

The fight drained out of Aarav all at once. His shoulders sagged, the weight of it all finally crushing him.

"I love Aimee," he said, his voice hoarse. "More than anything. And I'm done letting Dad—or anyone—decide my life for me. I don't care about his business, his expectations, or who he thinks I should marry. I'm done living for him."

Tia looked up, shaken.

"Aarav—"

"No," he said firmly. "I'm going to fix this. With Aimee. And if Dad has a problem with that, then that's his problem. I won't let him control me anymore."

Tia nodded slowly, guilt heavy in her chest.

"I'll talk to him," she said. "I'll try."

Aarav gave a humorless smile.

"Good luck."

He grabbed his jacket and stormed out, leaving Tia alone in the quiet apartment. She sat there long after the door closed, staring at the empty chair across from her, knowing she had crossed a line that could never truly be erased.

Later that night, back in her hotel room, Tia called Aarav again and again. He rejected every call—until, around two in the morning, he finally answered.

"What do you want now, Tia?" his voice was flat, exhausted.

"I didn't know," she cried. "I swear, I didn't know it would go this far. I thought I was helping. I thought if Aimee understood what she was up against, she'd try harder. I didn't realize it would push her away."

Aarav paced the room, running a hand through his hair.

"Try harder?" he snapped. "She's already been trying. I've been trying. But you—and Dad—you made her feel like she didn't belong. Like no matter how much we loved each other, it would never be enough. You made her feel like an outsider in my world."

"I'm sorry," Tia whispered, collapsing onto the bed, her face buried in her hands.

Aarav closed his eyes, the anger giving way to something heavier—grief. Not just for what was lost, but for how easily love had been undermined by fear and control.

Reflection

Sometimes love doesn't fall apart because two people stop caring—it fractures because too many voices interfere with what should have remained sacred. When family fear masquerades as protection, it can quietly teach someone that they don't belong. And once a person feels like an outsider in the relationship they're fighting for, walking away can feel less painful than staying and proving their worth every single day.

Chapter 28

Aarav knew he couldn't sit with the truth any longer. He had to find Aimee. He had to explain—everything.

The next morning, Aimee sat in the library, her head bent over a stack of books she wasn't really reading. Her eyes traced lines of text, but nothing stayed. Her mind was elsewhere—caught in memories of Aarav's strained expressions, his recent desperation, the growing guilt she carried for no longer being able to meet him where he needed her to be. She missed him—deeply—but something inside her had shifted. It wasn't just his anxious attachment or the pressure from his family anymore. It was something quieter, heavier.

She loved him. But she was beginning to fear that loving him meant losing herself.

Her phone buzzed beside her, pulling her out of her thoughts. Aarav's name flashed on the screen. She hesitated before answering.

"Aimee," his voice came through fast and unsteady. "I need to see you. Right now."

Her heart jolted. "Aarav, I'm—"

"Please," he interrupted. "It's important. I'm coming to you. Just... wait there."

The call ended before she could respond. Aimee's chest tightened. Something was wrong—she could hear it in his voice.

Fifteen minutes later, Aarav rushed into the library, scanning the room until his eyes found her. He looked exhausted—pale, restless, unraveling. He dropped into the chair across from her, his hands trembling as they landed on the table.

"We need to talk," he said.

Aimee searched his face. "What's going on?"

He inhaled sharply, trying to steady himself, but the words spilled out anyway.

"Tia told me everything. About my family. About my dad. About how she was sent here—to watch me. To make you feel like you'd never belong."

Aimee's breath caught. A chill ran through her.

"What?" she whispered. "Aarav... what are you saying?"

"She's the reason you pulled away, isn't she?" His eyes pleaded with her. "She told you my family would never accept you."

Aimee felt the truth settle heavily between them. She had wanted to protect him from it, to spare him the pain—but now there was no space left for silence.

"Yes," she said softly. "She told me. She told me we were too different. That your family would never choose me."

Tears filled Aarav's eyes as he shook his head.

"They don't get to decide who I love," he said, his voice breaking. "I don't care about their approval. I care about you. I love you."

Aimee swallowed, her emotions colliding.

"But you don't understand," she said quietly. "It's not just them. It's everything. You need so much from me, Aarav. And I'm trying—but I feel like I'm disappearing. Like I'm losing myself trying to keep you steady."

"I know," he whispered. "I know I've been too much. I've been terrified of losing you, and I held on too tight. But I'll change. I'll get help. I'll set boundaries—with my family, with my fear. Just... please don't leave me."

She looked at him and saw it all—the desperation, the love, the boy who was afraid of being abandoned. And she loved him. She truly did. But love wasn't quiet anymore—it hurt.

"I don't want to leave you," she said, tears pooling in her eyes. "But I don't know if I'm strong enough to carry all of this."

Aarav reached across the table, gently taking her hand.

"You don't have to carry it alone," he said. "We'll figure it out together. I'll fight for us. Please... don't give up on us."

Aimee squeezed his hand, torn between hope and fear.

"I don't know, Aarav," she whispered. "I just don't know."

Reflection

Sometimes love isn't questioned because it's weak—but because it's heavy. When one person is drowning in fear and the other is gasping for space, even the deepest connection can begin to feel unbearable. Loving someone should not require abandoning yourself, just as needing reassurance should not demand another person's identity. This is the moment where love asks a difficult question—not do you care, but can you grow without losing each other in the process?

Chapter 29

Over the next few days, Aarav did everything he could to show Aimee that he was serious about making things work. He drew firm boundaries with his family, making it clear that his relationship with her was his decision alone—and not something open for negotiation. He stopped the constant calling and texting, honoring the space she had asked for, even though it went against every anxious instinct in his body. For the first time, he also began therapy, finally confronting the anxiety and attachment wounds he had spent years avoiding.

From the outside, it looked like progress. Real change.

But inside, Aimee still felt unsettled.

Each moment they spent together carried an undercurrent of tension she couldn't ignore. No matter how hard Aarav tried, something felt misaligned—like two pieces that fit for a moment but never fully locked into place. The cultural distance between them felt heavier now, not lighter, and the shadow of his family's expectations lingered in the background of every shared silence.

One evening, sitting across from him in his dorm room, Aimee finally let the truth surface.

"Aarav," she said quietly, her hands clasped in her lap, "I see everything you're doing. I really do. But I'm still scared."

His chest tightened. "Scared of what?"

"Scared that we're forcing something that just... isn't meant to last," she admitted, her voice trembling. "I don't feel like I belong in your world. And I'm afraid one day we'll wake up and realize that love—no matter how real—wasn't enough."

Aarav felt the words hit him like a slow collapse. "But I love you," he said softly. "Isn't that enough?"

She looked at him, tears filling her eyes. "I don't know," she whispered. "I wish it were."

From that moment on, their relationship began to fray at the edges. Aarav tried harder—listened more, stepped back when he could—but Aimee's doubts refused to loosen their grip. Every interaction felt bittersweet: love wrapped tightly around guilt, affection shadowed by fear.

Sensing the growing distance, Tia tried to intervene. She spent more time with Aimee, hoping to undo some of the damage she had helped create.

"My family is difficult," Tia admitted one afternoon as they walked through campus. "But they'll come around eventually. They always do."

Aimee shook her head slowly. "It's not just them, Tia. It's me. I feel like I'm slowly disappearing—like I'm bending myself into something I don't recognize. I don't want to wake up one day and realize I gave up who I am for a relationship that couldn't survive reality."

Tia's heart sank. She could hear her own influence in Aimee's fear and hated herself for it. "You're not losing yourself," she said gently. "You're just afraid. And that's understandable. But what you and Aarav have—it's rare."

Aimee wanted to believe her. But the doubt had already taken root.

That night, unable to sit with her thoughts any longer, Aimee wandered through the quiet campus. The air was cool, the paths nearly empty, her mind swirling with questions she couldn't answer. She had tried to ground herself in dance, in routine, in distraction—but nothing quieted the ache inside her.

As she rounded the corner near the old fountain, a shadow shifted.

She stopped short.

"Aimee."

She looked up to see Aarav standing there, half-lit by the campus lights. His hands were buried deep in his pockets, his eyes filled with worry—and something else. Fear.

"What are you doing here?" she asked sharply, stepping back. "Were you following me?"

Aarav hesitated, guilt flooding his face. He hadn't planned to confront her like this. He had only seen her leave the dorm and felt something inside him panic.

"Yes," he admitted quietly. "I followed you. I didn't mean to—it just... happened."

Aimee stared at him, disbelief turning into anger.

"Do you even hear yourself?" she said, her voice tight. "This is exactly what I mean. You keep pushing. Watching. Holding on so tight that I can't breathe."

Reflection

Change doesn't always heal fear—especially when fear is rooted in loss. Aarav was learning to loosen his grip, but Aimee was learning something just as painful: that love alone cannot compensate for emotional safety. When one person's anxiety collides with another's need for space, even the purest intentions can feel like control. This moment isn't about blame—it's about recognizing when love begins to feel like pressure, and when holding on may be more damaging than letting go.

Chapter 30

Aarav's face crumpled at her words. He stepped closer, desperation cracking through his voice.

"I know," he said. "I know I've been too much. I just... I didn't know what else to do, Aimee. I'm terrified of losing you. You've been pulling away, and I can't stand it."

Aimee shook her head, frustration spilling over.

"I'm not pulling away because I want to," she said, her voice breaking. "You're suffocating me. I don't know how to be what you need all the time. I'm drowning under the weight of your expectations—and your family's." Her hands trembled. "I don't even recognize who I am when I'm with you."

Aarav went pale. "That's not what I want. I never wanted you to feel that way."

"But that's how I feel," Aimee said, her voice echoing into the quiet night. "I can't even think without worrying about how you'll react. Every time I ask for space, you panic. Every time I try to talk, it becomes about your fear of losing me." She paced, breath unsteady. "I love you—but I can't live like this."

Tears filled Aarav's eyes. He reached for her, voice trembling. "Please don't give up on us. I'll do better. I'm trying—really."

She stopped, turning toward him. Her heart ached at the sight of him like this—raw, unraveling.

"I don't know if I can keep doing this," she whispered. "I'm so tired."

He stepped closer, gently taking her hand.

"I love you," he said. "I don't want to lose you."

Something in his voice—the fear, the love—made her chest tighten. Despite everything, the pull between them was still there.

"I don't want to lose you either," she whispered.

Before she could stop herself, she closed the distance, fingers clutching his shirt. Aarav drew her in, cupping her face, and their lips met—desperate at first, then aching with all the words they couldn't say. The tension softened, giving way to longing and familiarity. They held each other as if letting go might break something fragile between them.

They parted briefly, foreheads touching.

"I love you," Aarav breathed.

"I love you too," she replied, tears shining in her eyes.

Hand in hand, they hurried toward her dorm, the night quiet around them. Once inside her room, the door closed softly, and the weight of everything they'd been carrying settled into a hush. Aarav's touch was gentler now—careful, reverent.

"Are you sure?" he asked softly.

"Yes," she said. "I want this. I want you."

They moved together without urgency, holding on, grounding themselves in the intimacy of being known. It wasn't about escape—it was about connection. In that space, they found each other again, if only for a while.

Later, they lay together in the dim light, her head resting on his chest, his arm wrapped around her. The world outside still felt uncertain—but in that moment, there was quiet, and there was love.

Reflection

Sometimes intimacy becomes a refuge—a pause where fear loosens its grip and two people remember why they chose each other in the first place. But closeness cannot replace safety, and passion cannot resolve patterns that need patience and healing. Love can feel like relief in the moment, yet still ask hard questions afterward: Are we choosing each other freely—or holding on because letting go feels unbearable?

Chapter 31

Aarav kissed the top of her head, his fingers threading gently through her hair.

"I don't want to lose this, Aimee," he whispered into the quiet. "I don't want to lose you."

Her heart ached at his words. She wanted to believe that love could be enough—that they could somehow outrun the doubts, the pressure, the fear of what lay ahead. But a part of her still trembled at the future, at everything unresolved between them. For now, she pushed those thoughts aside and held onto the warmth of his arms, to the fragile peace they shared in that moment.

"I love you," she whispered, pressing a soft kiss against his chest.

"I love you too," Aarav murmured, tightening his hold as sleep finally claimed them, as if their love itself was the only thing keeping them from breaking apart.

Morning arrived quietly. Sunlight slipped through the thin curtains of Aimee's dorm room, spilling warmth across the bed. Aimee stirred first, nestled against Aarav, the steady rhythm of his breathing grounding her for a fleeting second. The night before felt close—too close—and for a moment, she allowed herself to stay there, suspended in the comfort of his presence.

Then reality crept back in.

The arguments. The pressure. The weight of everything they hadn't solved.

A knot tightened in her stomach. She wanted to stay wrapped in this calm, but she knew it was only temporary.

Aarav shifted beside her, his arm tightening instinctively around her waist. His eyes fluttered open, and a soft, relieved smile crossed his face.

"Morning," he murmured, his voice rough with sleep.

"Morning," Aimee replied, returning the smile, though it didn't quite reach her eyes.

They lay there in silence, neither of them wanting to disturb the fragile stillness. But Aimee knew they couldn't avoid the truth for long.

"We can't keep doing this, Aarav," she said quietly.

His body stiffened. He turned to look at her, worry flooding his expression.

"What do you mean?"

"I mean we can't pretend everything is okay just because we had one good night." She sat up slowly, pulling the sheet around herself. Her voice trembled despite her effort to stay calm. "I love you. But nothing has actually changed. Your family, the pressure, your anxiety—it's all still there. And I don't know how much more I can take."

Aarav sat up too, panic creeping into his eyes.

"I'm trying, Aimee. I swear I am. I'll work on my anxiety. I'll deal with my family. I'll do whatever it takes."

She shook her head, tears welling.

"It's not just about you fixing things. It's about me. I'm losing myself. I've been trying so hard to fit into your world that I don't even recognize who I am anymore. I need space. I need to breathe."

The word space hit him like a blow.

"Space?" he whispered. "Are you saying you want to break up?"

"I don't know," Aimee admitted softly, looking away. "I just know that if something doesn't change, we're going to hurt each other even more."

He reached for her hand, desperation breaking through his voice.

"Please don't push me away. I can't lose you. Tell me what you need—I'll do it."

She gently pulled her hand back.

"I don't want to lose you either," she said, tears slipping free. "But I can't keep sacrificing myself to hold us together. I'm exhausted, Aarav. I'm so tired."

He stared at her, helpless, pain written across his face.

"I don't know how to fix this."

"I don't either," she whispered.

Silence settled between them, heavy and uncertain, like they were standing at the edge of something neither of them was ready to face. Finally, Aimee spoke again.

"Maybe we take it one day at a time," she said quietly. "Give each other space when we need it. Stop trying to force everything to be perfect."

Aarav nodded slowly. The idea terrified him—but he knew she was right. They had been clinging so tightly to each other that they'd forgotten how to stand on their own.

Reflection

Love can bring two people close, but closeness alone cannot heal what space is meant to reveal. Sometimes, stepping back is not a sign of giving up—it's an act of honesty. Growth asks for room, for breath, for patience. And only when two people can exist fully as themselves can love become a place of safety rather than survival.

Chapter 32

"Okay," he whispered. "One day at a time."

Aimee gave him a small, sad smile. "Yeah. One day at a time."

They stayed like that for a while longer, the morning light casting long shadows across the room as they silently held each other. Neither of them knew what the future held, but for now, they were still together—and that felt like something worth holding on to.

Over the next few days, Aarav and Aimee settled into a fragile peace, shaped by silent agreements and unspoken boundaries. It wasn't easy. There were moments when Aarav's anxiety hovered just beneath the surface—moments when Aimee caught his worried glances, his subtle attempts to reach out, to reassure himself that she was still there. But she needed the space, and he was trying—truly trying—to give it to her.

As Aimee threw herself into dance rehearsals, she found a different kind of solace in her time with Logan. The physicality of dancing—the way her body moved instinctively with the rhythm—helped clear her mind. Logan's easy, laid-back nature became an unexpected relief. He didn't demand anything from her, didn't expect her to be anything other than herself. For the first time in a long while, Aimee felt like she could breathe around someone.

Their rehearsals for the upcoming competition grew longer and more intense. Logan had always been a skilled dancer, but now there was an undeniable chemistry between them—something that went beyond technique. It wasn't that Aimee felt romantically drawn to him—at least, she didn't think so. But there was a comfort in their dynamic, a simplicity that stood in sharp contrast to the emotional complexity of her relationship with Aarav.

One afternoon, after a particularly grueling practice, they collapsed onto the studio floor, breathless and laughing. Logan stretched out beside her, his long limbs sprawled across the cool wooden surface. Turning his head toward her, a mischievous grin played on his lips.

"You know, you're really something, Aimee," he said, his voice light but sincere. "I don't think I've ever had a partner who pushes me as hard as you do."

Aimee smiled, a quiet swell of pride rising in her chest. "I guess that's what happens when you grow up with a dance instructor for a mom."

Logan chuckled. "Well, it shows. But seriously—I like working with you. I like... being around you."

The words lingered in the air, heavier than he probably intended. Aimee felt her pulse quicken slightly. She glanced at him, expecting the usual playful spark in his eyes, but instead found something softer—something genuine.

"Logan..." she began, unsure how to respond.

He shrugged, still smiling, though a hint of vulnerability crept into his expression. "I know you've got a boyfriend, and I respect that. I just wanted you to know. I like spending time with you. You make things uncomplicated."

The word uncomplicated stayed with Aimee. It captured exactly how she felt around Logan—no pressure, no expectations, just easy, natural companionship. He wasn't trying to undermine her relationship with Aarav. If anything, he was careful, respectful, never crossing boundaries or asking for more. Still, his presence felt like a quiet balm against the growing tension in her life.

Aimee smiled softly. "I like spending time with you too, Logan. You're a good friend."

His grin widened as he sat up and extended a hand to help her to her feet. "Come on. Let's get out of here before we get locked in."

As they walked back toward the dorms, their conversation light and effortless, Aimee found herself wondering why things couldn't feel this simple with Aarav. The thought filled her with guilt, as though she were betraying him just by allowing it—but the question lingered all the same.

Meanwhile, Aarav's anxiety had only grown in her absence. He had tried—he really had—to give her space, to respect her boundaries, to resist smothering her with his need for reassurance. But it was far harder than he had expected. Every delayed response, every mention of extended rehearsals sent his mind spiraling with the same fear: losing her.

He hated feeling this way. He knew it wasn't fair to Aimee, and he didn't want to be the insecure, clingy boyfriend. But the truth was, he couldn't help it. His love for her—and his fear of losing her—tightened around his heart like a vice. The more distance she created, the more desperate he became to pull her back.

And then there was Logan.

Aarav had never considered himself the jealous type, but something about Logan unsettled him. Maybe it was the ease with which Aimee spoke about him, the lightness that had slowly faded from their own conversations. Or maybe it was the uncomfortable truth that Logan seemed drawn to her—and that, in ways Aimee might not even recognize yet, she was drawn to him too.

Aarav tried to push those thoughts away, tried to trust her when she said Logan was just a friend. But every time his name came up, a knot of insecurity tightened in his chest. What if she was happier with Logan? What if Logan could give her the uncomplicated connection Aarav no longer could?

That night, alone in his room, Aarav stared at his phone for a long time before finally giving in. His fingers hovered over the screen before he pressed send.

Aarav: Hey, can we talk? I just... I miss you.

He waited, heart pounding, eyes fixed on the screen as the word delivered sat there—silent and unmoving.

Minutes passed.

No response.

Reflection

Sometimes distance doesn't begin with absence, but with exhaustion—the quiet kind that settles in when love starts to feel heavy instead of safe. Aimee wasn't searching for someone new; she was searching for herself. And Aarav, clinging tightly out of fear, didn't yet realize that love can't survive without space to breathe.

Chapter 33

H e tried to convince himself she was probably still at rehearsal, that there was nothing to worry about. But doubt crept in anyway, quiet and relentless. What if she was with Logan? What if she wasn't thinking about him at all?

Just as Aarav was about to send another message, his phone buzzed. His heart leapt—then sank.

Aimee: Hey, I'm still at practice. Can we talk tomorrow?

Tomorrow. Always tomorrow.

Aarav's hands clenched into fists. Before he could stop himself, he typed another message.

Aarav: Is it Logan?

A long pause followed.

Aimee: Aarav, what are you talking about?

He stared at the screen, his chest tightening. He could feel the familiar spiral beginning—the fight forming before either of them had said the wrong thing. But this time, he couldn't pull himself back.

Aarav: You're always with him. You spend more time with him than you do with me.

He knew it wasn't fair. He knew he was crossing a line. But the words poured out anyway, driven by fear—fear of losing her, fear of Logan, fear that he simply wasn't enough.

Another pause. Longer this time.

Aimee: Aarav, I told you before. Logan's just a friend. We're practicing for the competition. That's all.

But it didn't feel like "just a friend" to Aarav. Not when she laughed with Logan. Not when she seemed lighter, freer. Not when she spent hours in rehearsal while he sat alone, trapped in his own thoughts.

Aarav: I don't understand why you need him so much. Why can't you spend more time with me?

There was no immediate response. The silence stretched, heavy and suffocating, his heart pounding as his mind raced through worst-case scenarios.

Finally, the message appeared.

Aimee: We talked about this. I need space. You can't keep doing this.

And there it was—the quiet fracture in his chest, the confirmation of his deepest fear. She was pulling away. And no matter how hard he tried, he couldn't stop it.

The next day at rehearsal, Aimee tried to shake off the fight, but it followed her like a shadow. Logan noticed immediately, his brow furrowing as he watched her move through the routine with less energy than usual.

"You okay?" he asked during a break, handing her a bottle of water.

Aimee sighed, taking a long sip before shaking her head. "It's just Aarav. We had another fight last night."

Logan raised an eyebrow, concern settling into his expression. "About what?"

She hesitated, but the words slipped out anyway. "He thinks I'm spending too much time with you."

Logan blinked, then let out a quiet laugh—more surprised than amused. "He's jealous of me?"

Aimee nodded, frustration bubbling beneath the surface. "It's been getting worse. Every time I ask for space, he panics. Now he's convinced there's something going on between us."

Logan's expression softened. He reached out, resting a gentle hand on her shoulder. "You know I'd never try to come between you two. I respect your relationship. But... if I'm being honest, it sounds like he's putting a lot of pressure on you."

Aimee looked down at her hands, guilt weighing heavy in her chest. "He is. But it's not his fault. He gets anxious. He's always afraid I'm going to leave."

Logan's voice lowered, gentle and steady. "That sounds exhausting."

Her throat tightened. "It is. I love him... but sometimes, I feel like I can't breathe."

Logan didn't respond right away. His hand stayed on her shoulder, grounding, patient. "You deserve to feel free, Aimee," he said quietly. "To be with someone who trusts you."

She swallowed hard, emotions swirling in directions she didn't want to face. Logan wasn't wrong—she knew that. But the thought of walking away from Aarav, of letting go of the love they shared, felt unbearable.

She loved him.

Shouldn't that be enough?

Reflection

Love can exist without safety, and commitment can exist without peace. When fear replaces trust, even the deepest affection begins to feel like confinement rather than connection.

Chapter 34

B ut even as Aimee tried to steady herself, she couldn't deny the truth. With Logan, things felt easy. Uncomplicated. There was no fear, no pressure, no constant need to reassure him. And part of her—quiet but persistent—longed for that simplicity.

She tried to keep her focus on rehearsals, but Aarav's growing insecurities cast a shadow over everything. Every time her phone buzzed, a knot formed in her stomach, dread pooling in her chest as she braced herself for another message—another question, another accusation, another plea for reassurance.

It wasn't that Aarav was wrong to feel the way he did. She understood his fears. She understood how deeply he cared. But the constant push and pull was wearing her down, thinning her patience, exhausting parts of her she hadn't realized were already fragile.

Aimee hadn't intended for her time with Logan to become comforting. At first, it had been purely practical. They needed to train relentlessly if they wanted a real shot at the finals.

Logan—with his unyielding energy, flawless technique, and disciplined focus—had seemed like the ideal partner.

But somewhere along the way, rehearsals began to feel less like obligation and more like refuge. A pause from the emotional intensity that often came with loving Aarav.

Logan was steady. Present. When days stretched long and her body ached, he offered encouragement without expectation. Unlike Aarav—who often felt like a whirlwind of emotion—Logan was straightforward, easy to read. He didn't pry, didn't question, didn't demand explanations. He simply accepted her presence with a quiet, respectful warmth that slowly became comforting.

"Aimee, you've got to work on that left spin," Logan teased one afternoon, laughter echoing through the empty auditorium. "You nearly kicked me in the face."

She laughed, tension slipping from her shoulders. "I know, I'm sorry. I swear I'm not trying to ruin that flawless face of yours."

"Flawless, huh?" he raised an eyebrow, grin unwavering. "I'll take that."

They moved back into the routine, absorbed in the rhythm. When she stumbled, Logan's hand was there—steady, instinctive. When frustration crept in, he didn't analyze it or question her mood. He simply stayed. The simplicity of his presence seeped into her days, offering relief from the anxiety that often accompanied her time with Aarav.

With Logan, things didn't need explaining.

But of course, Aarav noticed.

At first, it was subtle—him stopping by the auditorium after practice, waiting quietly at the back. Arms crossed. Expression neutral. Watching.

But Aimee could feel it. Every laugh shared. Every glance held a second too long. Every time Logan's hand lingered after a lift, Aarav's jaw tightened. And each visit ended the same way—with him leaving more tense than before, jealousy settling deeper beneath the surface.

One evening, as Aimee and Logan wrapped up practice, Aarav appeared in the doorway. His face was carefully composed, but she recognized the darkness behind his eyes immediately.

"Aimee," he called, impatience threading through his voice. "We're supposed to get dinner. Remember?"

Her stomach dropped. She had lost track of time. Again.

She glanced at Logan, apology written across her face. He just shrugged, unbothered. "See you tomorrow?" he said lightly.

She nodded, gathering her things and hurrying toward Aarav.

The moment they were outside, his voice sharpened. "You two seem close."

"It's practice, Aarav," she replied, exhaustion edging her tone. "We're training for the finals. It's intense. Logan is... supportive."

His hand tightened around hers—just enough to be uncomfortable. "Supportive? That's not his role. You don't need him to be supportive."

"He's my partner," she said, steady but firm. "We have to work together."

He stopped abruptly, turning to face her. "Do you not see how close he's trying to get? Or do you just not care?"

Her chest tightened. She looked down, the familiar weight of his anxiety pressing between them. She wanted to soothe him, to say the right thing—but the words felt empty now. And the more he pushed, the stronger her instinct to pull away became.

Aarav's love was intense. Consuming. And she was beginning to feel like she was losing pieces of herself inside his need for reassurance.

In the days that followed, the tension only grew. Aarav's visits to rehearsals became more frequent, his presence heavy, watchful. She could feel his gaze tracking her movements, anger simmering just beneath the surface.

Logan noticed too.

After one particularly grueling session, he spoke gently. "You okay, Aimee?"

She looked up, startled. "Yeah. Why?"

"You seem tense," he said carefully. "And if this is about Aarav... I don't want to complicate things for you."

His words landed quietly but deeply. "It's not you," she said. "He just... gets jealous."

Logan exhaled slowly, eyes distant. "He's lucky to have you. But he shouldn't make you feel trapped. Love shouldn't feel like that."

She didn't answer. The truth sat too close to the surface.

The breaking point came during a routine lift—a difficult one, demanding absolute trust. Logan raised her, their movements seamless, eyes locked in silent coordination. For a brief moment, something passed between them—fleeting, unspoken, undeniable.

And that was when Aarav walked in.

Logan lowered her carefully, hands lingering at her waist as they steadied themselves. They looked up to find Aarav at the top of the stairs, fury written plainly across his face.

He stormed toward them.

"What is this?" His voice was low, controlled—and dangerous.

Aimee stepped away from Logan, her heart sinking. "Aarav, please. It's just practice. Not here."

Reflection

When love turns into vigilance, and reassurance becomes a requirement, connection begins to feel like captivity. And the quiet relief of being understood without explanation can be far more tempting than passion wrapped in fear.

Chapter 35

"Just practice?" he spat, his eyes blazing. "I can see what's happening, Aimee. Don't pretend I'm blind."

Logan sensed the hostility immediately and stepped in. "Aarav, relax. We're just practicing—"

"Stay out of this," Aarav snapped, his glare icy. "I'm talking to Aimee."

Logan raised his hands and took a step back, his tone steady. "I don't know what you think you're seeing, man, but we're dance partners. That's it."

Aarav's fists clenched, his face twisted with hurt and anger as he turned back to Aimee. His voice cracked despite his effort to stay composed. "Is that all, Aimee? Just a dance partner?"

"Yes," she whispered, her heart aching as she met his gaze. "That's all he is. But you're making this... so hard."

He stepped back, devastation written across his face. "I don't understand why you need him so much," he said quietly. "Why isn't what we have enough?"

Tears burned her eyes as she shook her head. "It's not about needing him. I just need space, Aarav. I need to breathe."

The hurt in his expression hardened into anger. "Fine," he said coldly. "Then maybe you should spend all your time with him."

Without another word, he turned and stormed away.

Aimee stood frozen as his footsteps faded, her chest tight and her thoughts spinning. Logan placed a gentle hand on her shoulder, a silent offer of support, but she pulled away softly, needing a moment alone.

The air felt heavy as the silence settled around her. She took a few shaky breaths, trying to steady herself. Logan remained nearby, watching her with quiet concern, unsure how to help without crossing a line.

"I'm sorry you had to see that," Aimee murmured, hugging her arms around herself.

"You don't need to apologize," Logan said gently. "It's clear things have been tense between you two for a while."

Her voice trembled. "I don't know how to handle it anymore. I love him, but he makes me feel like I'm suffocating. Every time he sees me with you, it's like he's searching for something to be angry about. And it's not fair—to you or to me."

Logan shook his head. "I can handle it. But this isn't about me. You shouldn't have to walk on eggshells around the people you care about. You deserve to be with someone who trusts you."

She nodded, unable to respond. His words struck painfully close to the truth, leaving her torn between relief and guilt. Loving Aarav had never been simple, but letting go felt impossible.

They returned to practice, quieter than before. Aimee tried to focus on the steps, on the rhythm, but her thoughts kept circling back to Aarav—his anger, his fear, the growing distance between them.

The next morning, Aarav texted her, asking if they could meet. The message was shorter than usual. She agreed.

They met on a quiet stretch of campus, the early air cool and still. Aarav was already there, pacing with his hands buried in his pockets. When he saw her, his expression softened, though worry lingered in his eyes.

"Hey," he said quietly.

"Hey," she replied, forcing a small smile.

For a moment, neither spoke. Then Aarav exhaled slowly. "I'm sorry about last night," he said. "I know I've been... intense. And I know it's been hard on you."

She looked down. "It's not just last night, Aarav. This has been building for a long time."

He nodded, running a hand through his hair. "I know. I just get scared. Every time I see you with Logan, it feels like I'm already losing you."

"I don't know how to keep reassuring you," she said softly. "Every time I'm with him, you question my loyalty. It's exhausting."

"I don't want to be like this," he whispered. "I'm trying. I swear."

She felt sympathy rise—but exhaustion outweighed it. "I know you're trying. But I can't keep sacrificing my peace just to calm your fears. That isn't love, Aarav."

His face crumpled, desperation flashing in his eyes. "I'm just trying to hold on to you," he said. "I don't know who I am without you."

Reflection

When fear replaces trust, love begins to feel like a burden instead of a refuge. No matter how deep the bond, a relationship cannot survive if one person must shrink themselves just to keep the other from falling apart.

Chapter 36

She reached out and took his hand. "I want to be with you too," she said softly. "But you have to let me breathe. You have to trust me."

Aarav looked down at their intertwined fingers and nodded, though the struggle was still etched across his face. "I'll try," he said quietly. "I promise I'll try."

They spent the rest of the day together, gentler than before, more careful with their words. Aimee could feel Aarav holding himself back, trying to rein in his anxiety, and she appreciated the effort. Still, a familiar fear lingered beneath the surface. She knew this wasn't something that could be fixed overnight.

As the days passed, Aimee found herself gravitating toward Logan during rehearsals. It wasn't intentional, but his presence felt calming in a way Aarav's often wasn't. With Logan, she could laugh freely, lose herself in the rhythm of the dance without carrying the emotional weight of someone else's fears.

Logan's straightforward nature slowly eased her tension. He wore his confidence lightly, pushing her to improve without judgment or expectation. Their connection felt easy and natural, grounded in movement and mutual respect. And there was something quietly reassuring about how he supported her—without asking for more than she was able to give.

One evening after practice, Logan handed her a water bottle and sat beside her, stretching his legs out.

"You're getting better at that lift," he said with a grin.

She laughed, taking a sip. "Thanks. Though I still feel like I'm going to fall every time."

"You won't," he said easily, nudging her shoulder. "Not with me around."

The warmth in his gaze made her look away, her cheeks flushing. She knew he didn't mean anything by it, but she had become more aware of the subtle ways he showed care—the quiet encouragement, the steady hands, the ease between them. It wasn't inappropriate, but it was comforting in a way she hadn't expected.

And she knew Aarav felt it too.

He came to rehearsals less often now, but when he did, the tension was unmistakable. Logan noticed it as well.

One evening, as they packed up, Logan hesitated. "Aimee, can I ask you something?"

"Of course."

"Is everything okay between you and Aarav?"

Her stomach tightened. "Why do you ask?"

"He seems... on edge whenever I see him," Logan said carefully. "I don't want to cause problems between you two."

She sighed, running a hand through her hair. "It's complicated. Aarav is dealing with a lot, and sometimes it affects how he sees things."

Logan nodded, understanding flickering across his face. "I get that. But you shouldn't have to walk on eggshells for someone else's peace of mind."

His words landed heavily. "I know," she said quietly. "But it's not that simple."

"I'm here if you ever need to talk," Logan added gently. "That's all."

Gratitude washed over her, followed closely by guilt. Nothing had crossed a line, yet the comfort she felt with him made her uneasy. She thanked him and left, her thoughts tangled and restless.

The turning point came during a late-night practice. They were working through a demanding routine that required absolute trust. As they moved together, Aimee felt free—fully present, unburdened, alive in a way she hadn't felt in weeks. Logan guided her smoothly, steady and reliable.

As the music ended, she caught sight of a familiar figure near the back of the auditorium.

Aarav.

His face was shadowed, but the anger beneath his gaze was unmistakable. He had seen them—the ease, the trust, the connection built through hours of shared effort.

He stormed over as soon as they finished.

"What is this?" he demanded, his voice low and tight with fury.

Aimee stepped back, startled. "Aarav, it's just practice. We were rehearsing."

Reflection

Sometimes the most dangerous distance in a relationship isn't physical—it's emotional. It forms quietly, in moments of relief, in places where you feel free instead of afraid. And once you notice the difference, it becomes impossible to ignore.

Chapter 37

He looked at Logan, his eyes burning with barely restrained anger.

"It doesn't look like practice to me."

Sensing the hostility, Logan stepped forward, his voice calm but firm. "Aarav, you're overreacting. We're just dancing."

"Stay out of this," Aarav snapped, his gaze never leaving Aimee.

The tension thickened instantly. Aimee felt Logan's eyes on her, silently urging her to speak, to stand up for herself. But before she could, Aarav's anger spilled over.

"You think I don't see what's happening here?" he said sharply. "I know you're getting close to him, Aimee. I'm not stupid."

Logan moved carefully, placing a hand on Aarav's shoulder in an attempt to de-escalate. "Aarav, you're reading too much into this. She's your girlfriend. Respect her. Trust her."

Aarav yanked away, his face twisted with rage. "Don't tell me how to handle my relationship!"

Aimee's stomach tightened as she looked between them, her heart pounding. Logan's calm only seemed to inflame Aarav further, his anger raw and unfiltered.

"Can we not do this here?" she pleaded softly, reaching for Aarav's arm. He pulled away.

"Why?" he shot back. "Why shouldn't we do this here, Aimee? You don't seem to have a problem spending all your time with him, so why does it matter where we talk?"

Logan's jaw tightened, but his tone remained steady. "Aarav, let's all take a step back. Let her breathe."

Aarav scoffed. "Oh, now you're her protector too? How convenient."

Aimee stood frozen, helpless as the argument spiraled. Logan's composure, the way he refused to rise to the bait, only pushed Aarav further into his fury.

"Aarav, please," she said again, firmer now. "You're blowing this out of proportion. We're just friends."

A bitter laugh escaped him. "Friends. Right. That's what you always say. But I see the way he looks at you."

Logan glanced at Aimee, sympathy clear in his eyes. "Aimee, maybe you should go. Let me talk to him."

"No," Aarav said immediately. "If anyone needs to leave, it's you. You're not part of this."

Logan met his gaze without flinching. "I am if this is about Aimee's well-being. I care about her, and I won't stand by while she's caught in the middle of this."

Aarav's fists clenched. For a moment, it looked like he might lash out. Instead, he laughed—a hollow, angry sound.

"You care about her? Is that it? That's why you're always here?"

"Yes," Logan said evenly. "I do care. But you're the one turning this into something it doesn't have to be."

The words struck deep. Aarav stepped closer, his voice low and venomous. "You think you can just replace me?"

Aimee moved between them, her heart racing. "Stop it, Aarav. This isn't you. This isn't us."

He looked at her then, pain and frustration colliding in his eyes. "Maybe it's not us anymore. Maybe you're happier with him."

The words cut deep. Tears burned behind her eyes. "That's not fair," she said, shaking her head. "You know it's not true."

"Do I?" he replied bitterly. "Because I don't feel like I know anything anymore."

The silence that followed was heavy and suffocating. Logan stayed quiet, respecting her space. Aimee met his eyes briefly, grateful for his restraint. He gave her a small, understanding nod.

"Aarav," she said softly, stepping closer. "Please. Let's go somewhere else and talk. Just the two of us."

He shook his head, hurt hardening into anger once more.

"What's the point? You've already chosen him."

She froze. "I haven't chosen anyone. You're the one I love. But I can't keep living like this—this constant doubt, this constant jealousy. It's tearing us apart."

For a moment, something shifted in his expression—regret flickering through the anger. But then his gaze landed on Logan again, calm and unmoved, and the rage returned.

Without another word, Aarav turned and stormed away, his footsteps echoing through the empty hall.

Aimee watched him go, her heart sinking as the reality of their fractures settled in.

Logan stayed beside her, quiet and steady, placing a gentle hand on her shoulder.

"I'm so sorry," she whispered, tears finally spilling over. "This is such a mess. And it's not fair to you."

Reflection

Jealousy doesn't always arrive as anger—it often arrives as fear. And when fear goes unchecked, it doesn't protect love; it slowly suffocates it, until even the people who care most can no longer breathe.

Chapter 38

Logan shook his head, his gaze warm and steady.

"You have nothing to apologize for, Aimee. You're carrying a lot right now. Just know I'm here—no matter what."

She offered him a small, grateful smile, but the ache in her chest didn't ease. Aarav's jealousy, his constant fear of losing her, had slowly turned into a kind of confinement—one built from guilt, obligation, and emotional exhaustion. And now, she wasn't sure they could ever return to what they once were.

In the days that followed, Aimee tried to reach out to Aarav, hoping to mend the widening distance between them. But each attempt ended the same way: unanswered calls, short replies stripped of warmth, his anger simmering just beneath the surface. No matter how carefully she chose her words, reassurance never seemed to reach him.

She continued rehearsing with Logan, though their interactions grew quieter, more cautious. Aimee was careful to keep everything strictly professional, yet she couldn't ignore the comfort she found in his presence. Logan's steadiness—his calm, uncomplicated way of being—stood in stark contrast to the volatility that now defined her relationship with Aarav.

One evening, after an especially draining rehearsal, Logan suggested grabbing a quick bite at a nearby café. Aimee hesitated. She knew how it would look to Aarav, how easily it could be misunderstood. But the thought of returning to her dorm—to the silence, the unanswered questions—felt heavier than the guilt.

They settled into a quiet corner, and for the first time in days, Aimee felt her shoulders relax. Logan talked about his family in Mexico, sharing lighthearted stories from his childhood. She laughed—genuinely laughed—and for a brief moment, the weight pressing on her chest lifted.

As the night wore on, conversation gave way to a comfortable silence. Aimee stared out the window, guilt stirring again. The peace she felt now was something she hadn't experienced with Aarav in a long time.

"You're thinking about him," Logan said softly.

She nodded. "I feel like I'm betraying him just by being here."

Logan reached across the table, resting his hand gently over hers.

"You're not betraying anyone. You're allowed to have friends. You're allowed to feel okay."

Her voice wavered. "He's been through so much. I feel responsible for him—like I have to stay, no matter what it costs me."

Logan's expression softened. "Caring about someone doesn't mean disappearing for them. You matter too, Aimee."

His words struck deeper than she expected. She knew he was right, but releasing the guilt—the sense of obligation—felt impossible.

They walked back toward campus in silence. As they neared the dance hall, Aimee's steps slowed. A familiar figure stood in the shadows, rigid and waiting.

Aarav.

Her heart sank. One look at his face told her everything—he had seen them together. The hurt, the anger, the disappointment were unmistakable.

"Aimee," he said tightly.

Logan paused, sensing the tension. "I'll give you space," he murmured, offering her a supportive nod before stepping away.

Aarav watched him go, his jaw clenched. When he turned back to her, pain and resentment flickered in his eyes.

"So this is what you do now? Spend your nights with him?"

"It's not like that," she pleaded. "We were just talking. He's my friend."

"Your friend," he repeated bitterly. "Funny how he's always there when I'm not."

She stepped closer. "Aarav, please. I love you. But I can't keep living like this—constantly afraid of upsetting you."

"Then why do you keep running to him?" he shot back. "Why is he the one who makes you laugh? Who you turn to when you're falling apart?"

Her voice broke. "Because you're not there anymore. You're so consumed by fear—by losing me—that you're pushing me away. I feel like I'm suffocating."

For a moment, his anger cracked. Vulnerability flickered across his face. But it hardened again just as quickly.

"I'm not the one who changed," he said coldly. "You did."

Then he turned and walked away.

Aimee stood frozen, watching him disappear into the night. Something painful but undeniable settled inside her.

She loved Aarav.

But love—on its own—wasn't enough when it required her to lose herself.

As the echoes of their argument faded, exhaustion washed over her. She grieved what they had been, even as she accepted what they were becoming. Logan's presence had only sharpened the contrast—how strained everything felt now, how far she had drifted from the version of herself who once felt whole.

With Logan, life felt lighter. Not romantic—just free. And that realization frightened her more than anything else.

Reflection

Love should expand you, not confine you. When staying means shrinking, even the deepest affection begins to feel like a quiet loss.

Chapter 39

The next day, Aimee found herself back in the dance studio for their usual practice. Logan greeted her with a quiet smile, as if he sensed the storm still churning beneath her calm exterior. His ease was both comforting and unsettling—a sharp contrast to the emotional weight she carried whenever she thought about Aarav.

"Aimee, you okay?" Logan asked gently. "You don't have to explain anything, but I can tell it's been rough."

She leaned against the wall, exhaling slowly. "It's just... complicated. Sometimes it feels like Aarav and I are barely holding on. And at the same time, I don't know how to let go."

Logan nodded, thoughtful. "That kind of history isn't easy to walk away from." He paused before adding carefully, "But maybe... space isn't about letting go. Maybe it's about not hurting each other more."

"Space is the last thing he wants," Aimee said softly. "He's terrified that if he loosens his grip even a little, I'll disappear."

Logan's voice stayed calm. "Sometimes when someone's afraid of losing something, they hold on so tightly they don't realize they're crushing it."

His words settled heavily in her chest.

They moved into rehearsal, and little by little, Aimee let the rhythm take over. Dance had always been her release—movement turning emotion into something she could survive. Logan was steady beside her, his touch grounded and respectful, offering support without demand. It made her feel safe in a way that was both soothing and disorienting.

That day, the routine felt sharper, more charged. Their movements flowed with a quiet intensity, an unspoken understanding passing between them. Logan didn't ask for explanations. He didn't expect reassurance. He was simply present.

As they practiced a difficult lift, their eyes met. There was admiration there—mutual, sincere—but also something warmer, more human. Aimee felt it and quickly looked away.

"Logan," she said quietly, "I don't want to make things worse with Aarav. But... thank you. For being here."

He held her steady, his voice gentle. "I'm here because I want to be. And if all I ever get to be is your friend, that's enough."

Her chest tightened. Gratitude and guilt tangled together, impossible to separate.

When practice ended, they lingered outside the studio, conversation drifting easily. Then Logan's gaze flicked past her.

Aimee turned—and saw Aarav standing a few steps away. His posture was rigid, his fists clenched, his expression a mix of hurt and anger that made her stomach drop.

Logan acknowledged him with a brief nod. "Aarav."

Aarav ignored him, his focus locked on Aimee. "I thought you needed time alone," he said tightly. "Didn't realize that meant spending it with him."

"It's not what you think," she said quickly. "We just finished practice."

"Right," Aarav replied bitterly. "Because it's always just practice."

Logan stepped in, calm but firm. "Aarav, we're friends. I respect Aimee, and I respect that you're together. But it's not fair to put her in the middle of this."

Aarav's eyes darkened. "Stay out of it. You don't know what we've been through."

"Maybe not," Logan said evenly. "But I do know she deserves to feel safe."

That was enough.

Aarav stepped closer, anger cracking through his restraint. "You really think you're the good guy here?"

Aimee moved between them, her voice steady despite the pounding of her heart. "Enough. This isn't helping anyone."

She turned to Aarav. "I told you I need space. And every time you confront me like this, you make it harder to breathe."

His face fell. "So you're choosing him?" he asked quietly.

The pain in his voice nearly broke her.

"I'm not choosing anyone," she said, tears burning behind her eyes. "But I can't stay in something that's suffocating me. I love you, Aarav—but love shouldn't feel like this."

For a moment, he looked like he might collapse under the weight of her words. Then he turned away.

"Fine," he said, his voice hollow. "If that's what you want."

He walked off without looking back.

Aimee stood frozen, guilt and heartbreak crashing through her at once. Logan rested a gentle hand on her shoulder, grounding her.

"I'm sorry," she whispered.

"You don't need to be," Logan said softly. "Standing up for yourself takes courage."

They stood there in silence, the air heavy with everything left unsaid. Aimee knew she had done what she needed to do—but knowing didn't make it hurt less.

She was caught between two worlds, two very different kinds of love. And for the first time, she understood that choosing herself might be the hardest choice of all.

Reflection

Sometimes the bravest thing you can do is admit that love, when tangled with fear, can slowly become a cage—and that choosing yourself isn't betrayal, but survival.

Chapter 40

Over the next few days, Aimee tried to ground herself in routine—dance, repetition, movement—anything that resembled normalcy. She continued practicing with Logan, grateful for the quiet steadiness he brought into her days. He never pushed, never questioned her choices. In his presence, she felt something rare and unfamiliar: calm.

Yet Aarav's absence lingered like a bruise she couldn't stop touching. She knew he was hurting. She understood that his jealousy was rooted in fear, that his insecurities ran deep. But she also knew she couldn't be the only one fighting to keep their relationship alive.

One evening, after a long rehearsal, she and Logan decided to grab coffee. They found a small café tucked away from campus, its warm lighting and soft music offering a temporary refuge from the tension that had come to define her life.

As they sat across from each other, Aimee felt her shoulders finally relax. Logan didn't fill the silence with questions or expectations. He simply listened. And before she realized it, she was telling him everything—the exhaustion, the guilt, the impossible pressure of trying to keep everyone happy.

"You don't have to carry all of this alone, Aimee," Logan said gently. "Sometimes it's okay to let go. Sometimes it's okay to just be."

His words settled quietly inside her. Logan had become something she hadn't meant for him to be—a safe place. A steady presence when everything else felt fragile and uncertain.

But the tension between Aimee and Aarav was far from easing.

Despite her decision to create space, Aarav couldn't silence the jealousy clawing at him. Each day without her felt heavier than the last. Watching her grow closer to Logan only fed his fear that he was losing her—for good.

Aimee felt herself being pulled in opposite directions. With Aarav came history, love, heartbreak, and a deep emotional bond that refused to loosen its grip. With Logan came ease. Lightness. Breathing room. The contrast became impossible to ignore as Logan respected her boundaries while every interaction with Aarav turned into an emotional battle.

One evening, after an exhausting rehearsal, Aimee and Logan stayed behind to fine-tune the final details of their performance. Their chemistry onstage had sharpened through weeks of relentless practice. Logan admired her openly, though he never crossed a line. His glances lingered, his touch during lifts warm and careful—but restrained.

As they wrapped up, Aimee noticed a familiar figure standing at the entrance.

Aarav.

He was still, half-shadowed by the dim lights, watching them with an intensity that sent a chill through her. Logan followed her gaze and nodded politely.

"Hey, Aarav," Logan said, easy as ever. "We're just finishing up."

Aarav didn't respond. He stepped closer, his jaw tight, eyes flicking between them.

"I see you two have been getting... close."

The bitterness in his voice made Aimee wince. "Aarav, please. Not now. We're just practicing."

"Practicing?" Aarav scoffed, his gaze sharpening on Logan. "I don't think I've ever seen a practice that looks like this."

Logan raised his hands slightly, calm but firm. "You're reading into it. Aimee and I are dance partners. That's all."

"That's easy for you to say," Aarav shot back, his voice cracking despite himself. "You're not the one watching someone else get close to the person you love."

His eyes flicked to Aimee—raw, wounded.

"Maybe if you trusted her," Logan said quietly, "you wouldn't feel like you had to question her every move. She deserves that much."

The words landed hard.

Aarav stepped forward, fists clenched, something dark flashing across his face. "And who are you to decide what she deserves? You think you can just walk in and take her away?"

The air thickened with tension, and Aimee felt her heart pound as the fragile balance between them threatened to shatter completely.

Reflection

Sometimes love doesn't fall apart because it disappears—but because fear grows louder than trust, and holding on begins to hurt more than letting go.

Chapter 41

Logan met Aarav's gaze steadily.

"This isn't about taking her away," he said calmly. "It's about giving her the freedom to choose what she wants. Maybe you need to let her do that—without pressure."

Aimee stepped between them, her voice strained with urgency.

"Aarav, please. Logan isn't the problem. We need to talk—but not like this."

Aarav looked at her, and for a brief moment, something in his expression softened. But the anger hadn't left him.

"Why him, Aimee?" he asked, his voice raw. "Why does it feel like you can be yourself around him, but not around me?"

She swallowed hard, the weight of his words settling in her chest.

"It's not about choosing him over you," she said quietly. "I just... I need space. I don't want to feel trapped."

"I don't want to trap you," Aarav said, his voice breaking. "I just don't want to lose you."

Before she could respond, Logan stepped forward again.

"If you really care about her," he said, "then listen to what she's asking instead of fighting it."

Aarav's face hardened, fury flaring in his eyes.

"And maybe you should stop pretending you're just a friend."

Logan's jaw tightened, but he held his ground.

"Maybe if you gave her space, you'd see she doesn't need anyone else to make her happy. She just needs to feel free."

Something in Aarav snapped.

Without warning, he lunged forward and shoved Logan hard. The movement was sudden—violent. Logan stumbled backward, his foot catching the edge of the stairs leading down from the rehearsal stage.

Time seemed to slow.

Logan's arms flailed as he lost his balance, shock etched across his face before he disappeared over the edge, tumbling down the staircase.

"Aarav—!" Aimee screamed.

She rushed forward, her heart slamming in her chest as she reached the stairs. Logan lay at the bottom, stunned, clutching his arm, his ankle already swelling.

Aarav stood frozen at the top, horror flooding his face.

"Aimee, I—"

"How could you?" she shouted, her voice shaking with fury. "What were you thinking?"

She didn't wait for an answer.

Aimee ran down the stairs and knelt beside Logan, her hands trembling as she assessed him.

"Logan, are you okay?"

He forced a weak smile through the pain.

"Guess that wasn't my best landing."

Her throat tightened. She glanced up briefly, meeting Aarav's stricken expression—but only for a second. The anger in her chest was too fierce to ignore.

"We need to get you to the clinic," she said softly.

She helped Logan sit up, supporting his weight carefully. She didn't call for Aarav. Didn't look at him again.

Aarav followed them down the stairs, helpless, reaching out instinctively to help—but Aimee brushed his hand away sharply. The look she gave him then—cold, wounded, furious—cut deeper than any words could have.

At the campus clinic, Aimee took charge immediately. She helped Logan onto a cot, her movements controlled despite the slight tremor in her hands. She called for the nurse and stayed by his side as his ankle was examined and wrapped.

Aarav lingered near the doorway, silent, his hands buried in his pockets, regret written across his face.

"Thanks, Aimee," Logan said once the nurse finished. "Looks like I'm out of practice for a while."

She managed a small smile.

"We'll get you back on your feet. I'm just glad you're okay."

As the nurse left, Aimee picked up a cloth and gently dabbed a scrape on Logan's forehead. Her touch was careful, compassionate. Unburdened.

Aarav watched from the doorway, a hollow ache spreading through his chest. She hadn't spoken to him once. Hadn't even acknowledged him. And he knew he deserved it.

That look—her calm, her focus, the way she tended to Logan—it used to be his.

He couldn't stand it anymore.

Aarav turned and walked out of the clinic, his footsteps echoing down the hallway. Outside, the cold night air hit him like a shock. He stumbled to a bench and collapsed onto it, burying his face in his hands.

His shoulders shook as the sobs broke free.

He had crossed a line.

And now, he could feel it—

he was losing her.

Reflection

Sometimes love doesn't fall apart quietly.
Sometimes it breaks in a moment you can't take back.

Chapter 42

After a few minutes, Aarav sensed someone behind him. He looked up quickly, wiping at his eyes.

Aimee stood a few steps away, her arms crossed tightly over her chest, her expression guarded—unreadable.

"Aarav," she said, her voice calm but resolute, "I think it's best if you leave."

The words landed heavier than he expected. His mouth opened, searching for something—anything—that might undo what had already happened. But all that came out was a broken whisper.

"I'm sorry, Aimee. I never meant for any of this to happen."

She shook her head slowly. Her eyes held disappointment more than anger, and somehow that hurt worse.

"That's the problem," she replied. "You didn't mean for it to happen—but it did. You let your jealousy take control, and someone got hurt."

He swallowed hard, his instinct to reach for her battling the look in her eyes. There was pain there. And distance.

"I can't be around you right now," she said quietly. "I need space. And Logan needs support. So please... just go."

Aarav hesitated for a moment, taking her in as if committing her face to memory. Then, without another word, he turned and walked away, his steps heavy as he left the campus grounds.

The guilt followed him like a shadow.

For the next two days, he didn't return to the university. He stayed locked in his room, ignoring his phone, avoiding the world, replaying that moment over and over until it hollowed him out completely.

Meanwhile, Aimee stayed by Logan's side.

She helped him adjust to his injury, steadying him as he learned to move carefully again. Despite the pain, Logan's spirit remained intact. He cracked jokes, complained theatrically about being "grounded," and teased her about slipping too easily into the role of caretaker.

"You didn't sign up to be a nurse when you joined the dance team, did you?" he joked one evening, his smile easy.

Aimee rolled her eyes, unable to hide her own smile.

"I think it was buried somewhere in the fine print."

Logan chuckled, then reached out and gently patted her hand.

"Seriously, Aimee. Thank you. I don't know what I'd do without you."

The sincerity in his voice warmed her. For a moment, the weight she'd been carrying eased. Being with Logan was uncomplicated—no pressure, no unspoken expectations. He didn't question her intentions or ask her to reassure him. He simply accepted her presence.

As the days passed, and she helped Logan through his recovery, she found comfort in the rhythm of their time together. They spent hours in the studio, slowly adapting their routine to his limited movement. She noticed small things she hadn't before—the way his eyes lit up when he laughed, the quiet encouragement he offered without making it feel like a demand, the steadiness that put her at ease.

It wasn't romantic. At least, not to her.

Logan was simply someone who made her feel seen, respected, and safe. And right now, that was enough.

Aarav returned to campus late one evening, each step weighed down by dread—and a fragile hope that maybe, somehow, he could still make things right.

He hadn't seen Aimee since the night of the accident. The silence between them had carved something hollow inside his chest. But he couldn't avoid it any longer. He needed to face her. Needed closure—whatever form that took.

He found her in the dance studio, alone, moving through a routine under the soft glow of dimmed lights. She hadn't noticed him enter. Her eyes were closed, her body fluid and focused, moving with a grace that stilled him where he stood.

Watching her stirred everything at once—love, admiration, regret. She looked peaceful. Whole. So different from the guarded version of her he carried in his memory.

She finished the final movement and opened her eyes.

Their gazes met.

The warmth on her face faded instantly, replaced by careful distance.

"Aarav," she said quietly. She didn't step toward him.

"Can we talk?" he asked, his voice thick, barely steady.

Reflection

Sometimes the hardest distance
   isn't physical—
   it's the space created by a single moment you can't undo.

Chapter 43

She hesitated, then nodded slowly, gesturing toward the wall of mirrors along the studio. Aarav followed her, and they sat with a few feet of space between them. For a moment, neither spoke. The silence pressed in on them, heavy with everything they were afraid to say.

Finally, Aarav broke it.

"Aimee... I'm so sorry," he said, his voice unsteady. "For Logan. For pushing him. For hurting you." He swallowed hard. "I don't know why I let things get so out of control."

Aimee stared at the floor, her fingers twisting together in her lap.

"I know you didn't mean to hurt anyone," she said quietly. "But intention doesn't change the damage, Aarav. Every time I think we're moving forward, your jealousy pulls us back. I don't know how much more I can give."

His chest tightened. "I know I've been too much," he said quickly. "I'm trying to work on it—I really am. But you have to understand... I love you. And sometimes it feels like I'm losing you, like I'm losing myself."

She looked up at him then. Her expression softened, but her eyes stayed guarded.

"Love shouldn't feel like this," she said. "It shouldn't make me feel like I'm walking on eggshells, or constantly proving that I'm still here. I'm exhausted, Aarav. I can't fight your fears and mine at the same time."

The words landed hard.

"So what are you saying?" he asked, his voice barely holding together.

Tears slipped down her cheeks.

"I don't want to lose you," she whispered. "But I don't want to keep losing myself either. I can't keep sacrificing my peace just to make you feel safe."

Something sharp flickered across his face—hurt, fear, anger he didn't mean to show.

"So I'm just too much for you?" he asked, the words spilling out before he could stop them.

She shook her head, wiping her tears.

"No. But I feel like I'm disappearing in this relationship. Like I'm always trying to be what you need, always reassuring you, always shrinking myself so you don't panic." Her voice cracked. "I don't think I can do that anymore."

Aarav looked away, jaw clenched, his hands tightening together.

"I never wanted you to feel trapped," he murmured. "I was just scared. Terrified of losing you."

"I know," she said softly. "But love is supposed to feel safe. Somewhere along the way, we lost that."

The silence returned—thicker this time, filled with finality.

Aarav looked back at her, his eyes shining with regret and desperation.

"So... is this it?" he asked.

Her shoulders slumped. Fresh tears fell.

"I think it has to be," she said quietly. "For both of us."

The words shattered something inside him.

Without thinking, he reached for her, cupping her face, brushing away her tears.

"Please," he whispered. "Just one more chance. I'll get help. I'll change. Don't leave me."

She closed her eyes, her hands rising to his face as she leaned into his touch—then gently shook her head.

"This isn't about you changing for me," she said softly. "I think we both need to learn how to be okay on our own. We need to let go... to heal."

The truth hung between them.

"I don't know how to let you go," he admitted, his voice breaking.

She gave a sad, tender smile, her fingers tracing his cheek.

"Neither do I," she whispered. "But sometimes the hardest thing is the right thing."

They leaned into each other one last time, foreheads pressed together, holding on as if love alone could undo the damage. Every unspoken word, every regret, every memory poured into that final embrace.

They both knew—

It was goodbye.

Reflection

Sometimes love doesn't end
    because it disappears—
    it ends because holding on
    starts to hurt more
    than letting go.

Chapter 44

As they pulled apart, Aimee wiped her tears with trembling fingers.

"This doesn't mean I don't love you, Aarav," she said softly. "I think... I always will. But we need to be okay apart before we could ever be okay together."

He nodded, even as his heart broke all over again. He leaned in and pressed a final kiss to her lips—slow, lingering, heavy with love and regret. She kissed him back, both of them holding on for a few stolen seconds longer than they should have.

When they finally stepped away, Aimee took a shaky breath and forced a small, sad smile. She reached for his hand one last time, their fingers intertwining as if muscle memory refused to let go.

"I think..." she whispered, "...you should go."

Aarav nodded. Each step toward the door felt like something inside him was splintering. He turned back once, memorizing her—standing alone in the soft light, her face etched with love, pain, and quiet finality.

The door closed behind him with a gentle click, the sound echoing down the empty hallway, marking the end of something they had both fought to hold onto.

He walked away, every step a dull ache in his chest, his mind spinning, his heart shattered.

Back in the studio, Aimee sank to the floor. She pulled her knees to her chest as the reality of their goodbye settled over her, tears spilling freely now that she was alone.

It was over.

The months that followed passed in an uneasy quiet. Aarav and Aimee still occupied the same spaces, but they became nearly invisible to one another—crossing crowded hallways, shared classes, and mutual friends without exchanging a glance. The breakup left a raw ache in both of them, one neither could fully outrun. Still, each was determined to rebuild, piece by piece, into someone stronger—someone less likely to break the next time love demanded too much.

For Aimee, healing came slowly. She threw herself into her classes, her friendships, and her dance, trying to fill the hollow space Aarav had left behind. Logan remained a steady presence—supportive, respectful, never crossing lines. Their bond deepened not through romance, but through companionship, laughter, and shared discipline on the dance floor. With graduation approaching, her focus sharpened. She dreamed of joining a professional dance company, a future that stretched beyond Columbia University and anchored her in possibility.

Aarav, meanwhile, immersed himself in his studies with quiet determination. He ignored graduation flyers and celebrations, focusing instead on research papers and job applications. To his surprise, he secured a promising offer with a tech company in New York City—a chance at independence, a clean start. And yet, even with the promise of a new beginning, regret followed him everywhere.

Sometimes, across campus, he caught glimpses of Aimee—a flash of her hair as she laughed with friends, the light in her eyes when she danced at student events. Each time, his chest tightened. She seemed to be thriving, or at least projecting a version of herself untouched by his memory. He told himself that was a good thing. She deserved happiness without the weight of his fears.

Still, late at night, doubts crept in. He wondered if she ever thought of him, if any part of her missed what they'd shared. He pushed the thoughts away, reminding himself that this was the work he had to do—learning how to live without her voice, her warmth, her reassurance. It felt like amputating a part of himself, but he faced each day with a resolve he hadn't known he possessed.

As graduation neared, the campus buzzed with bittersweet anticipation. Students planned their futures, balancing excitement with nostalgia, aware that their time together was ending. Aarav received invitations to graduation parties, as did Aimee, but neither attended any where the other might be present. It was as if, without ever speaking about it, they had agreed to create separate worlds—parallel, but no longer touching.

Reflection

Some endings don't explode.
   They fade—
   quietly, painfully—
   until two people who once meant everything
   learn how to exist
   without each other.
   And sometimes,
   that is the bravest kind of love there is.

Chapter 45

Logan noticed the change in Aimee as graduation drew closer—the way her gaze lingered on passing clouds outside classroom windows, the quiet pauses that settled over her while everyone else celebrated. He didn't ask questions. He didn't push. Instead, he stayed where he was—steady, unobtrusive, a quiet anchor reminding her that even in her loneliness, she wasn't alone.

The day before graduation, Aarav stood in his dorm room, packing the remnants of his college life into cardboard boxes. His future in the city waited just beyond these walls, but his hands moved slowly, distracted. As he cleared his desk, his fingers brushed against a framed photograph from sophomore year.

It was him and Aimee—laughing, faces pressed together, caught in a moment of unfiltered joy. They looked younger. Softer. Untouched by the weight that would eventually fracture them. A bittersweet smile crossed his face as he stared at it, memories pressing hard against his chest.

After a long moment, he slipped the photo into a box. He couldn't throw it away. But he also couldn't leave it where it could keep breaking him.

He was nearly finished packing when his phone rang, the sharp sound cutting through the quiet room. Aarav glanced at the screen, his breath hitching when he saw his father's name. His father rarely called directly, and something about the timing sent a chill through him.

He answered, his voice cautious.

"Hello, Papa?"

There was silence on the line—too long, too heavy. Then his father spoke, his voice low, trembling beneath the weight of words he was struggling to say.

"Aarav... I need you to sit down."

Aarav's heart began to pound. "What's wrong?" he asked quickly. "Is everything okay?"

His father inhaled sharply, and when he spoke again, his voice broke.

"It's... it's your mother," he whispered. "There was an accident. She didn't... she didn't make it."

The world tilted.

The words echoed in Aarav's ears, colliding with one another until they no longer sounded real. The room seemed to drain of air as his knees buckled and he collapsed into the desk chair, his hands shaking violently.

"No... no, Papa," he stammered, his voice cracking. "That's not—this can't be true."

"I know, beta," his father said softly, grief heavy in every syllable. "But it is. We need you here. I need you to come home."

Images flooded Aarav's mind—his mother's gentle hands, her laughter filling the house, the calm wisdom in her voice whenever life overwhelmed him. She had always been his constant. His safety. And now, that foundation was gone.

"Papa..." he whispered, tears spilling freely now. "I'll come. I'll be there as soon as I can."

His father thanked him quietly, but Aarav barely registered the words. He ended the call and sat motionless, staring at the phone in his trembling hands, trying to understand a world in which his mother no longer existed.

Somehow—through numbness more than strength—he booked a flight for later that night. Missing graduation, the day his mother had spoken about with such pride, felt cruel. But it was insignificant compared to the ache hollowing out his chest.

His suitcase lay half-packed on the bed. He couldn't bring himself to finish. Instead, he sat there in silence, fists clenching and unclenching, as memories surfaced without mercy.

Reflection

Grief doesn't arrive gently.
  It interrupts.
  It dismantles futures mid-sentence
  and leaves people standing in rooms
  that no longer feel real.
  And sometimes,
  loss doesn't wait for closure—
  it arrives when life is already asking
  everything from you.

Chapter 46

As the hours crept by, Aarav moved on autopilot. He stuffed clothes into his suitcase, gathered his documents, and prepared to leave, his mind detached from his body. Every movement felt slow and heavy, as if he were wading through quicksand, weighed down by grief he couldn't yet fully grasp.

When he finally stepped outside, the cool evening air struck his face, jolting him briefly into the present. He paused, looking out over the familiar campus grounds, their outlines blurred through his tear-filled vision. Everything felt unreal, as though he were walking through a dream he couldn't wake from.

This place had been his home for so long—a space where he had built friendships, discovered himself, met Aimee, learned what love felt like, and then what heartbreak could do. And now, he was leaving it behind.

As he walked toward the car waiting to take him to the airport, he passed the building that housed Aimee's dorm. The sight of it tightened something in his chest. For a moment, the urge to call her overwhelmed him—to tell her what had happened, to hear her voice, to lean into the comfort she once gave him so effortlessly.

But he stopped himself.

He knew he couldn't open that door—not now. He couldn't let her see him like this, hollowed out and breaking. And so he kept walking, his heart heavy, his thoughts muted, leaving behind the fragments of a life he wasn't ready to say goodbye to.

At the airport, seated in the waiting area among strangers and the low hum of boarding announcements, Aarav felt suspended in a vacuum. The plastic chair beneath him felt distant, the surrounding voices muffled and indistinct. Grief had numbed him, wrapping him in a strange, quiet detachment.

And yet, despite himself, his thoughts drifted to Aimee.

Memories rushed in, sharp and vivid, crashing over him before he could stop them. He closed his eyes and let himself fall into them.

He remembered the first night they stayed up too late, squeezed together on the narrow couch in his dorm room, talking about everything and nothing at all—philosophy, music, the universe. He could still hear her laughter, light and unguarded, see the way her eyes sparkled as she teased him about his strange taste in movies. They had fallen asleep mid-conversation, her head resting on his shoulder, his arm instinctively wrapped around her. It was the first time he had felt something close to pure happiness.

Then there were the early mornings they spent together, sneaking out to the quiet park just off campus. They'd sit in silence with steaming cups of coffee, watching the sun rise. Aimee would tilt her face toward the light, eyes closed, breathing deeply as if trying to memorize the moment. In those quiet hours, he had come to know the softness she rarely showed—a gentleness she protected fiercely. And each morning, he'd feel an overwhelming need to keep her close, to shield her from anything that might hurt her.

He remembered the small, thoughtful ways she loved him—notes slipped into his backpack, clumsy attempts at cooking his favorite meals. One night stood out clearly. She had surprised him with a homemade dinner, trying desperately to make it perfect. The pasta was undercooked, the sauce far too salty, but she watched him anxiously, biting her lip, waiting for his reaction. He had smiled and told her it was perfect, savoring every bite because he knew how much effort she'd put into it. They'd laughed until their stomachs hurt, leaning into each other as though nothing else existed.

There was the night they danced by the lake, their quiet sanctuary on campus. Aimee had insisted she couldn't dance, but he'd taken her hand anyway, guiding her gently into a slow rhythm. They barely moved, swaying under the moonlight, her head resting against his chest. He could feel her heartbeat, steady and real, could sense the vulnerability she rarely allowed anyone to see. That night, he had felt something settle deep inside him—a closeness beyond words, as if they were woven together by something unbreakable.

He remembered their study sessions too, which almost never stayed focused. She would huff in frustration over a difficult equation while he leaned over her shoulder to help. But he'd inevitably find himself distracted by the crease between her brows, the way she bit the end of her pencil when she concentrated. She'd catch him staring and roll her eyes, though he always noticed the smile she tried to hide. Their teasing would take over, laughter filling the room, the air between them charged with something neither of them dared to name back then.

Reflection

Love doesn't leave all at once.
   It lingers in ordinary places—
   in dorm rooms, quiet parks,
   half-burnt dinners, and unfinished conversations.
   And sometimes,
   in the middle of loss,
   memory becomes both a refuge
   and a wound—
   a reminder of what once felt like home.

Chapter 47

Then there were the spontaneous road trips—the reckless joy of abandoning plans and driving for hours with no destination in mind. One weekend, they had driven to a nearby town just to see an art exhibit Aimee had read about. They wandered through the museum hand in hand, her commentary making him laugh so hard he had to stifle it to avoid disturbing other visitors. Afterward, they explored the town without direction, sharing inside jokes and quiet glances that carried the comfort of being deeply known.

And of course, there was the intimacy—the moments that lived beyond words. The quiet nights spent tangled in each other's arms, breathing in the stillness, feeling a closeness he hadn't known was possible. Her laughter during those moments was softer, more vulnerable, as if she were letting him into parts of herself no one else had seen. Those nights felt magical—filled with whispered confessions and gentle kisses, a world where only they existed, safe and whole in each other's embrace.

Aarav felt a tear slip down his cheek, unnoticed at first.

The realization struck him all at once—that those moments were no longer his present, that he was sitting alone in an airport surrounded by strangers, the one person he wanted beside him unreachable. He opened his eyes and took in the bustling terminal, the movement and noise amplifying the hollow ache spreading through his chest.

He hadn't told her he was leaving. Hadn't reached out in his grief. The thought gnawed at him relentlessly. He knew he was heading back to a home that no longer held the same warmth or sense of belonging. And yet, as he thought of Aimee, he realized something painful and true—he had left a part of himself with her, even if she never knew it.

He wiped his tears and tightened his grip around his boarding pass, steadying himself. In all the time they had shared, he hadn't told her just how deeply he loved her, how profoundly she had changed him. That realization hurt most of all—that his words had gone unsaid, left suspended between them like unfinished sentences.

When his flight was finally called, Aarav rose to his feet. Each step felt heavier than the last as he moved toward the gate, memories of Aimee etched into his heart, carrying him forward even as it felt like he was leaving everything he had ever held dear behind.

Reflection

Some loves don't end with closure.
  They end with silence—
  with words unsaid,
  goodbyes postponed,
  and memories that travel farther than we ever can.

Chapter 48

Mumbai greeted Aarav with a familiar, bittersweet chaos. The scent of damp earth from the fading monsoon rains lingered in the air, blending with the metallic edge of the city's relentless motion. As the car wove through crowded streets, neon-lit hoardings loomed overhead, advertising luxury apartments and the latest Bollywood releases. This city had once been home—but now, it felt foreign. The noise outside was nothing compared to the storm inside his chest.

The car pulled up to the Mehta mansion, a sprawling colonial estate standing defiantly against Mumbai's ever-evolving skyline. The house was just as he remembered—grand, immaculate, and heavy with formality. It had never felt warm. Never felt gentle.

His father, Rajesh Mehta, stood at the entrance with his hands clasped behind his back. He looked older than Aarav remembered, his hair threaded with gray, the lines on his face etched deeper by grief. As Aarav stepped out of the car, the weight of loss settled fully into the space between them.

"Aarav," Rajesh said, his voice steady but subdued.

There was no hug. No hand on the shoulder. Only a restrained nod—an acknowledgment more than a welcome.

"It's good you came back," his father continued. "We need you here now."

Tia, on the other hand, broke immediately.

She rushed toward him and wrapped her arms around him, clinging as though letting go might undo everything. Her shoulders shook as she whispered, "I'm glad you're here. I don't know how we're supposed to get through this without you."

Aarav held her, his arms tightening around his sister as the weight of her words settled deep in his chest. Together, they walked inside the house, but the hollow feeling followed him. His mother's absence was everywhere—in the silence of the corridors, in the stillness of the rooms, in the way her laughter no longer softened the edges of the house. The warmth she once carried through these halls had vanished, leaving behind something cold and cavernous.

The days that followed blurred into one another, marked by rituals, prayers, and an endless stream of condolences. Family friends and business associates filled the house, offering sympathy with solemn faces while quietly assessing Aarav—measuring how he would fit into the family's carefully maintained image.

Rajesh Mehta remained composed throughout it all, accepting condolences with a polite, practiced smile. Tia fought back tears, retreating whenever the weight became too much. Aarav stood somewhere between them, trying to be present while grief pressed relentlessly against his chest, heavy and suffocating.

On the fourth evening after his arrival, Rajesh summoned Aarav to the study.

The room smelled faintly of old books and polished wood, unchanged by time or tragedy.

"You know this business is yours to take over," his father said, his tone firm, stripped of softness. "Your mother wanted this too. She always believed you'd bring fresh ideas—modernize what we've built."

Aarav's gaze drifted to the family portraits lining the wall. His father stood at the center of each frame, imposing and resolute. Beside him, his mother's gentle smile softened the rigidity, her presence a quiet counterbalance.

"I'll do what I can," Aarav replied, his voice low and weighted.

Rajesh's jaw tightened. "There's no room for what you can. You need to commit fully, Aarav." He leaned forward slightly. "This is your home now. This is your legacy."

Legacy.

The word landed like a burden across Aarav's shoulders. His life in New York—his independence, his dreams, Aimee—felt impossibly distant, like something that had belonged to another version of himself. Here, there was no space for uncertainty or grief.

Here, he was the dutiful son.

The heir.

The future of the Mehta name.

And with that realization, Aarav understood something deeply unsettling:

his life was no longer his own.

Reflection

Grief does not always arrive as tears.
  Sometimes it arrives as responsibility—
  as expectations placed gently but firmly on broken shoulders,
  asking us to become someone else
  before we've had time to mourn who we were.

Chapter 49

Aarav fell into a routine.

His mornings were consumed by factory visits—walking production floors, reviewing operations, and meeting employees who regarded him with a careful mix of respect and curiosity. Afternoons passed in conference rooms and offices, buried in financial reports, contracts, and negotiations. No matter where he was, his father's presence lingered—unspoken but constant—casting a shadow over every decision, every measured response.

But nights were the hardest.

His bedroom, preserved almost exactly as it had been during his childhood, felt less like a place of rest and more like a mausoleum. He would sit by the window, watching the city stretch endlessly beneath him, its lights flickering like distant stars. Inevitably, his thoughts drifted to Aimee.

He could still hear her laughter—soft, unguarded. He could still feel the warmth of her hand in his, the quiet intimacy of moments where words were unnecessary. He wondered what she was doing now. Whether she had moved on. Whether she ever thought of him at all.

The memories came without warning: the way sunlight caught in her hair, the gentle pressure of her fingers laced through his, the peace he'd felt simply being beside her. And with each memory came the same ache—sharp, familiar, inescapable.

It was during one of Rajesh's meticulously planned business dinners that Aarav first met Ruchika.

The evening was held in honor of Mr. Malhotra, a longtime business partner of the Mehtas, who arrived accompanied by his daughter. Aarav had little interest in the event. By then, he had perfected the art of polite detachment—offering the right smiles, the right nods, the right responses to satisfy his father.

Ruchika arrived late, apologizing softly for traffic as she entered the room.

She wore a navy-blue sari embroidered with delicate silver thread, her hair swept back into an elegant bun. There was an ease to the way she moved—quiet confidence, controlled and self-assured. She didn't demand attention, yet the room seemed to adjust around her presence.

"Aarav," Rajesh said, gesturing toward her, a note of approval unmistakable in his voice. "This is Ruchika. Mr. Malhotra's daughter. She runs their PR division—and does exceptional work."

Ruchika extended her hand. "It's a pleasure to meet you, Aarav. I've heard a lot about you."

"All good things, I hope," Aarav replied, offering a courteous smile as he shook her hand.

"That depends on who you ask," she said lightly, a mischievous glint in her eyes.

Her wit caught him off guard.

Throughout the evening, Ruchika remained effortlessly composed. She spoke with ease about current affairs, shared stories from her work, and navigated conversations with a natural fluency that made people lean in rather than feel spoken at. Once or twice, she even managed to make Aarav laugh—an unfamiliar sound these days.

He noticed it, even if he didn't acknowledge it.

There was no denying her charm. Still, Aarav kept his walls firmly in place.

Over the following weeks, Ruchika became a recurring presence in his life. Rajesh ensured her inclusion—at family gatherings, business lunches, and formal dinners—each invitation carrying an unspoken intention. Aarav was acutely aware of his father's quiet maneuvering, yet he found it difficult to resist Ruchika's company.

She was intelligent, articulate, and possessed a disarming sense of humor. More than that, she never pushed—never pried.

Chapter 50

One evening, during a smaller, more relaxed dinner at the Mehta residence, Ruchika found Aarav standing alone on the balcony.

She approached quietly, two cups of tea in her hands, her footsteps barely audible against the marble floor.

"Mind if I join you?" she asked.

"Not at all," Aarav replied, gesturing to the empty chair beside him.

They sat in comfortable silence for a moment, the city lights stretching endlessly below them, flickering against the night sky.

"You don't seem like someone who enjoys these kinds of gatherings," Ruchika said eventually, her tone observant rather than critical.

Aarav let out a quiet laugh. "What gave me away?"

"The way you disappear to the balcony every chance you get," she said with a small smile. "You're not very subtle."

He smirked. "Fair enough. It's never really been my thing."

She took a slow sip of her tea, her gaze thoughtful. "You seem... distant," she said gently. "Like you're here physically, but your mind is somewhere else."

Her words caught him off guard.

"It's been a lot lately," Aarav admitted after a pause. "Adjusting to life here. Stepping into my father's world. It's... overwhelming."

"I can imagine," Ruchika said softly. "Living under someone else's expectations can feel suffocating."

Something in her voice struck a nerve. For the first time in weeks, Aarav felt seen—not as an heir, not as a responsibility, but as a person quietly struggling to hold himself together. He glanced at her, noticing a depth beneath her composed exterior, the subtle understanding of someone who had fought her own battles.

Despite Ruchika's growing presence, Aarav's nights remained haunted by thoughts of Aimee.

He often found himself scrolling through old photos on his phone—moments frozen in time, memories that brought both comfort and pain. He knew reaching out to her would only reopen wounds neither of them was ready to face, but the longing lingered, stubborn and unresolved.

As the weeks passed, his relationship with his father grew increasingly strained. Rajesh's expectations were relentless, each conversation layered with pressure and unspoken demands. Aarav felt less like a son and more like a vessel—molded, directed, shaped to serve a legacy that left no room for his own identity.

Chapter 51

One night, after a particularly heated argument, Aarav wandered through the streets of Mumbai with no destination in mind. The city buzzed around him—horns blaring, voices overlapping, life moving forward without pause. The chaos mirrored the storm inside him.

For the first time in weeks, he stopped fighting it.

He stood beneath a flickering streetlight and let the tears fall, grief and frustration spilling out unchecked. He felt trapped—caught between the life his father demanded and the life he had left behind, neither offering the peace he desperately needed.

The next morning, Aarav woke to find a note placed neatly on his bedside table.

Aarav,

We have a board meeting at 11 a.m. Be punctual and prepared.

We will be discussing the expansion strategy.

It wasn't surprising.

Rajesh had a way of issuing commands disguised as expectations, never once asking if Aarav was willing—or ready—to shoulder them. Aarav exhaled slowly, crumpled the note, and tossed it aside. The weight pressing down on him felt heavier with each passing day, the walls closing in tighter than ever.

The meeting itself was long and tense, filled with numbers, projections, and polished presentations that blurred together. Aarav stared at the screen as charts shifted from one slide to the next, his mind drifting far from the boardroom.

His life had become a checklist of obligations, a performance of responsibility. And somewhere along the way, he had lost sight of who he was beneath it all.

After the meeting ended, Rajesh pulled him aside.

As his father spoke—firm, composed, already outlining the next expectation—Aarav felt something quietly fracture inside him. The grief he carried had no space to breathe here. His mother's absence was treated like a pause in operations, not a wound still bleeding beneath his ribs. There was no moment to mourn, no permission to falter. Only forward motion. Only responsibility.

He realized then that loss did not always arrive as chaos or collapse. Sometimes it came disguised as structure. As routine. As a life that continued moving so relentlessly that it left no room for the person he had been before everything broke.

In New York, he had lost love.

In Mumbai, he was losing himself.

And standing there, nodding as his father spoke, Aarav understood something with painful clarity: grief wasn't just about who he had lost—it was about who he was being asked to become in the aftermath. Someone stronger, quieter, more obedient. Someone shaped by duty rather than desire.

He wondered, not for the first time, whether survival meant endurance...

or whether it required choosing himself before there was nothing left to choose.

Sometimes grief does not demand tears.

Sometimes it demands identity.

And the hardest loss is not what we leave behind—but who we are expected to replace ourselves with in order to move forward.

Rajesh's gaze sharpened as he studied his son.

"You were distracted," he said, his voice clipped. "You can't afford that, Aarav. You need to be focused. People are watching you now."

"I'm trying," Aarav replied, his jaw tightening as he struggled to keep his frustration in check.

"Trying isn't enough," his father snapped. "You're a Mehta. That comes with responsibilities."

The conversation ended as abruptly as it had begun, leaving Aarav standing there with a familiar mix of anger and helplessness churning in his chest. He walked out of the office building, needing air, needing distance—needing something he couldn't quite name.

That evening, obligation pulled him to one of the company's charity events. The lights were warm, the music polished, the smiles carefully practiced. Aarav felt detached from it all—until he noticed Ruchika.

She stood surrounded by a group of children, laughing as they eagerly showed her their artwork. There was an ease to her presence, a quiet sincerity that cut through the artificial buzz of the event. Without fully realizing it, Aarav found himself drawn toward her.

"You look like you need a drink," Ruchika said when she noticed him, handing him a glass of sparkling water.

"Is it that obvious?" he asked, managing a small smile.

"Only to someone who knows what it feels like to wear a mask," she replied gently.

They drifted toward the edge of the garden, away from the noise. Aarav leaned against the railing, his eyes fixed on the city lights stretching endlessly into the distance.

"Sometimes," he admitted quietly, "I feel like I'm suffocating. No matter what I do, it's never enough for him."

Ruchika studied him for a moment before speaking. "I understand. My father is the same. He believes my life should revolve around the company—that I should want exactly what he wants." She paused, her voice softening. "But I have my own dreams. My own plans."

"What do you want?" Aarav asked, genuinely curious.

She smiled, a hint of longing in her expression. "I want to start an NGO for underprivileged children. I want to make a difference that actually feels meaningful to me. But that's not the future my father imagines."

Her honesty unsettled something in him. In her words, Aarav saw a reflection of his own quiet struggle—two people suspended between duty and desire, expected to inherit lives they never fully chose.

"You should do it," Aarav said, surprising himself with the certainty in his voice. "Don't let anyone else decide your life for you."

Ruchika looked at him, her expression soft but knowing.

"You should take your own advice, Aarav."

Reflection

Sometimes the people who see us most clearly are the ones walking the same invisible line—between who we are expected to be and who we quietly hope we still have the courage to become.

Chapter 52

That night, Aarav lay awake long after the house had gone quiet.

The Mehta mansion, once filled with his mother's gentle presence, now felt cavernous and cold. The walls carried the weight of legacy—every portrait, every antique clock, every carefully curated silence reminding him of who he was supposed to become. He stared at the ceiling, his chest tight, his mind refusing to rest.

Ruchika's words echoed in his head.

You should take your own advice.

It unsettled him more than he wanted to admit.

For weeks now, he had been telling himself that returning to Mumbai was the right thing to do—that stepping into his father's world was responsibility, not surrender. He had framed it as maturity, as growth. But lying there in the dark, stripped of distraction, the truth pressed in on him with uncomfortable clarity.

He wasn't choosing this life.

He was disappearing into it.

Every day, he wore the role expected of him—the obedient son, the future heir, the composed executive. He spoke when spoken to, agreed when agreement was demanded, nodded through meetings that left him feeling hollow. His father saw progress. The board saw promise. Everyone seemed satisfied.

Everyone except him.

The hardest part wasn't the workload or the pressure—it was the quiet erosion of self. The slow realization that his own wants had begun to feel irrelevant, almost selfish. That somewhere along the way, he had stopped asking himself what he needed, replacing the question with what was required of him.

And then there was Aimee.

Her absence lived inside him like a second heartbeat—constant, aching, impossible to ignore. He had told himself that letting her go was the right thing, that love shouldn't feel like fear, that stepping away was an act of respect. But grief had a way of rewriting logic. In the stillness of the night, he wondered if he had given up too easily—or if he had held on too tightly, until love had turned into desperation.

He hated that both could be true.

With Aimee, he had felt alive—terrified, yes, but alive. With her, emotions were raw and unfiltered, joy and pain woven tightly together. Here, in Mumbai, everything was controlled. Predictable. Safe.

And unbearably empty.

Ruchika had seen through him so quickly. Not his success, not his polish—but the fracture beneath it. The part of him still aching for autonomy, still grieving not just his mother or Aimee, but the version of himself that once believed life could be shaped by choice rather than obligation.

He turned onto his side, staring out the window at the sleeping city.

Was this what adulthood was supposed to feel like—endurance instead of fulfillment?

Was responsibility meant to come at the cost of identity?

Or had he simply mistaken sacrifice for strength?

For the first time since returning home, Aarav allowed himself to ask the question he had been avoiding:

If no one were watching... who would I choose to be?

The thought frightened him more than his father's anger ever had.

Because the answer might change everything.

Reflection

Sometimes the deepest conflict isn't between two people—but between the life we are praised for living and the one that quietly waits for us to claim it.

Chapter 53

Later that night, Aarav sat alone on the balcony of his room, the city stretched out beneath him in a haze of lights and distant noise. Ruchika's words lingered in his mind, looping quietly, persistently. He stared up at the stars, their faint glow reminding him of how far away everything he loved now felt.

And then, without warning, Aimee slipped back into his thoughts.

He remembered their impromptu dance practices—the way she would laugh whenever he missed a step, her eyes bright with mischief. He remembered how she used to rest her head against his shoulder during quiet moments, how her presence alone had grounded him in a way nothing else ever had.

One memory rose above the rest.

A rainy evening in New York.

They had been walking back from a small café when the sky opened up, soaking them within minutes. Instead of running for cover, Aimee had spun in the rain, arms stretched wide, laughter echoing through the empty street. Aarav had watched her, mesmerized, before stepping into the rain himself. They had danced there—careless, soaked, breathless—their clothes clinging to their skin, their hearts beating in perfect rhythm.

The ache in his chest tightened until it almost hurt to breathe.

He missed her in a way that words couldn't contain. And the thought of her moving on—building a life without him—cut deeper than he cared to admit.

The next morning, Aarav was summoned to the study again. This time, his father's tone was calm, deliberate—almost strategic.

"I've been thinking about your future," Rajesh said, pouring himself a glass of whiskey despite the early hour. "You're settling in well. But there's something else we need to address."

Aarav felt his muscles tense.

"I spoke with Mr. Malhotra," Rajesh continued. "We both agree it would be beneficial for you and Ruchika to spend more time together. She's intelligent, capable, from a respected family. She would make an excellent partner."

Aarav's stomach churned. "Dad, I'm not interested in marriage."

"This isn't just about marriage," Rajesh said sharply. "It's about alignment. Ruchika understands our world—our responsibilities. She would be an asset. To you. To this family."

"I'm not ready," Aarav said, his voice rising despite himself.

"You don't need to be ready," his father snapped. "You need to be practical. You can't keep living in the past. It's time to move forward."

Something inside Aarav snapped.

"You don't get to decide how I live my life," he shot back.

Rajesh's eyes hardened. "As long as you live under this roof, you will do what's best for this family."

Aarav stormed out, his heart pounding, the walls of the house suddenly feeling unbearably tight. He needed air. Distance. Space to think.

That evening, he found himself by the waterfront, the cool breeze cutting through his restless thoughts. The waves moved steadily, indifferent to the storm inside him. His father's words replayed in his mind. So did Ruchika's calm presence. And always—Aimee.

His life felt like a series of impossible choices, each one pulling him further away from the person he wanted to be.

His phone buzzed.

A message from Ruchika.

I hope you're okay. If you ever want to talk, I'm here.

He stared at the screen for a long moment before typing a single word.

Thanks.

It wasn't rejection. It wasn't invitation. Just honesty.

For the first time, he felt a faint flicker of something unfamiliar—a quiet understanding, a connection that didn't demand or overwhelm. But even that was eclipsed by the weight of his past, by memories of Aimee that refused to loosen their grip.

Chapter 54

Aarav threw himself into work after that—long days, longer nights. He avoided his father when he could and kept his interactions with Ruchika polite, minimal. He didn't blame her for his father's expectations, but her presence was a constant reminder of the life being planned for him—a life he hadn't chosen.

One evening, Rajesh hosted a formal dinner at the mansion. Business associates filled the rooms alongside their families—tailored suits, elegant gowns, champagne flutes raised in practiced smiles. Aarav attended out of obligation, retreating quickly to the bar at the edge of the room.

As he poured himself a second glass of whiskey, a familiar presence appeared beside him.

Ruchika.

She wore a midnight-blue saree that complemented her quiet elegance, her posture effortless, composed. She seemed untouched by the performance required of the evening—calm, observant, self-possessed.

And for a brief moment, Aarav wondered—not what his father wanted for him—but what it would mean to choose something for himself.

"Let me guess," she said, raising an eyebrow. "You're counting down the minutes until you can leave."

"Something like that," Aarav replied, swirling the amber liquid in his glass.

She smiled, leaning casually against the bar. "I don't blame you. These events are exhausting. At least the whiskey's decent."

He chuckled, surprised by her candor. "Didn't take you for a whiskey person."

"There's a lot you don't know about me, Aarav Mehta," she said, her eyes glinting with mischief.

As the night wore on and the guests slowly began to disperse, Aarav found himself stepping outside into the garden, his drink still in hand. He needed air—space to think, to breathe. To his surprise, Ruchika followed him, a glass of whiskey cradled loosely in her fingers.

"Escaping again?" she asked, her tone teasing.

"Maybe," he admitted. "And you?"

"Escaping you," she said with a smirk. "Looks like that didn't work."

They sat on a stone bench near the fountain, the steady sound of water filling the silence. For a moment, neither spoke. Then Ruchika broke the quiet.

"Why do you hate this so much?" she asked softly.

He turned toward her, caught off guard.

"All of it," she continued, gesturing toward the house behind them. "The business. The expectations. The life your father has planned for you. Why does it bother you so deeply?"

Aarav exhaled slowly, running a hand through his hair. "Because it isn't my life. It's his. His dreams. I just happen to be the one expected to live them."

Ruchika nodded, her expression thoughtful. "I understand that. My father's the same way. I used to fight it constantly—until I realized it was only draining me. Now I choose my battles more carefully."

"And which ones are you fighting now?" he asked, genuinely curious.

She smiled, the humor fading into something quieter. "Trying to figure out who I am without all of this. Trying to find something that feels real."

Her words landed heavier than he expected. For the first time, Aarav saw her not as part of his father's design, but as someone navigating her own confinement—intelligent, self-aware, and quietly restless.

The night deepened, and they remained in the garden, talking about nothing and everything. Without realizing it, Aarav began to open up—about his mother, his time in New York, even Aimee.

Ruchika listened without interruption, without judgment. She didn't try to fix anything. She simply let him speak.

By the time the bottle was empty, the tension he usually carried had softened. His laughter came easier, unguarded in a way it hadn't been for months.

"You know," Ruchika said, her words just slightly slurred, "you're not nearly as insufferable as I expected."

"High praise," Aarav replied, grinning.

Reflection

Sometimes the first person who truly sees you isn't the one who knows your history—it's the one who recognizes your silence. And in a life built on expectations, even one honest conversation can feel like oxygen.

Chapter 55

They sat in companionable silence for a moment, the night air cool against their skin. The sounds of the city faded into the background, leaving only the quiet between them. Without thinking, Ruchika leaned her head against Aarav's shoulder.

"You're warm," she murmured, her voice barely audible.

Aarav stiffened, his heart suddenly racing. He wasn't sure what to do, unsure whether to pull away or stay still. But something about the moment felt unexpectedly right. Slowly, he relaxed, allowing her to rest there.

As the alcohol's haze began to fade, Aarav became acutely aware of how close they were—the warmth of her body, the soft rhythm of her breathing. He turned his head slightly and looked down at her. Her eyes were closed, her expression calm, almost vulnerable.

"Ruchika," he said softly.

She opened her eyes and met his gaze. The space between them felt charged, heavy with something unspoken. For a long moment, neither of them moved. Then, almost unconsciously, Aarav leaned in, their faces only inches apart.

Before the moment could cross into something else, Ruchika pulled back. Her expression shifted—uncertain, conflicted.

"We shouldn't," she said quietly, her voice trembling just slightly.

Aarav nodded, guilt washing over him. "You're right. I'm sorry."

"It's not your fault," she replied quickly. "It's just... complicated."

They remained there for a while longer, the moment dissolving, though the tension lingered between them—unresolved, unspoken.

In the days that followed, Aarav and Ruchika continued to spend time together. Their connection deepened in ways neither of them had anticipated. It wasn't romantic—at least not yet—but it was undeniable.

Ruchika became a steady presence in Aarav's life. Her humor, her warmth, the ease with which she spoke her mind—all of it felt grounding. She challenged him, gently but persistently, to think beyond his father's expectations, to consider what he actually wanted for himself.

And Aarav, despite himself, found that he cared for her in a way he hadn't planned.

One evening, as they sat on the terrace overlooking the city, its lights stretching endlessly before them, Aarav turned to her.

"Do you ever think about leaving?" he asked.

"All the time," she admitted. "But I don't think running away is the answer. I think..." She paused, choosing her words carefully. "I think we have to learn how to live on our own terms—even if it's within the constraints of this life."

Her words stayed with him long after she left that night.

Reflection

Sometimes connection doesn't arrive as passion—it arrives as understanding. And sometimes the most dangerous closeness isn't desire, but the quiet realization that someone sees you in ways you didn't know you needed.

Chapter 56

The moment that changed everything arrived on a rainy evening.

Aarav and Ruchika had attended a fundraiser together, an obligation neither of them had questioned. On the drive back, the rain intensified, and somewhere along the deserted stretch of road, the car sputtered before coming to a complete stop.

They stared at each other for a beat—then burst out laughing.

"Looks like we're stranded," Ruchika said, shaking her head as rain streaked down the windshield.

"Perfect timing," Aarav replied. "Of course this would happen today."

They spotted a small roadside café nearby and ran for it, laughing as the rain soaked their clothes. By the time they stepped inside, both were breathless, hair damp, cheeks flushed.

"You look like a drowned rat," Aarav teased, brushing water from his jacket.

"And you look like a wet dog," Ruchika shot back, rolling her eyes.

They ordered tea and slid into a corner booth. The café was warm and dimly lit, the sound of rain tapping against the windows creating an intimacy that neither of them acknowledged. As they talked—about nothing and everything—the space between them felt different. Charged. Something unspoken had been building for weeks, and now it hovered between them, impossible to ignore.

When the rain softened into a drizzle, they stepped back outside. Aarav walked Ruchika to her car, hesitating as she reached for the door.

"Goodnight," she said softly, her eyes meeting his.

"Goodnight," he replied.

Neither of them moved.

Before he could talk himself out of it, Aarav leaned in and kissed her. It was tentative at first, uncertain, as if he were testing a line he'd promised himself not to cross. Then Ruchika kissed him back—and all hesitation dissolved.

The kiss was raw and unrestrained, filled with emotion they had carefully avoided naming. Weeks of restraint, of proximity without permission, collapsed into that single moment.

When they finally pulled apart, both of them were breathless.

"This changes everything," Ruchika whispered, her voice unsteady.

"I know," Aarav said quietly. "But maybe... maybe it's time something did."

The next morning, Aarav woke with an unfamiliar heaviness in his chest. His mind replayed the kiss, Ruchika's words echoing over and over—This changes everything.

Before he could make sense of what that meant, his phone buzzed.

Come to the study. We need to talk.

His mood sank instantly.

Conversations with his father were never casual. Still, he dressed and made his way downstairs.

Rajesh Mehta sat behind his massive mahogany desk, flipping through documents. The room smelled faintly of cigars, the walls lined with books Aarav suspected had never been opened.

"Sit," Rajesh said without looking up.

Aarav lowered himself into the leather chair opposite him.

"We've secured the deal with the Kapoor family," Rajesh began. "They'll be investing in the new project. Ruchika's father played a key role in finalizing it."

Aarav nodded, sensing where this was heading.

"I want you to take a more active role in managing this partnership," Rajesh continued. "And I want you to get closer to Ruchika. She's a good girl. She'll bring stability into your life."

There it was.

"I'm already working with her," Aarav said carefully.

"Not just professionally," Rajesh replied, finally lifting his gaze. "Personally. She's exactly the kind of woman you need."

Aarav clenched his fists beneath the desk. "My personal life isn't something you get to manage."

Rajesh's expression hardened. "You're my son. Your choices reflect this family and this business. Don't forget that."

Aarav stood abruptly, the tension suffocating. "If that's all, I have work to do."

Rajesh didn't stop him as he left, but Aarav felt the weight of his father's expectations pressing into his back.

That evening, Aarav found himself standing in his mother's room.

It had been left untouched since her death—a quiet shrine frozen in time. The faint scent of her perfume lingered in the air. Her favorite books sat neatly stacked on the bedside table, exactly where she had left them.

The silence was unbearable.

For the first time, Aarav felt the collision of everything at once—grief, duty, desire, guilt. Love he hadn't healed from. A future being arranged for him. A choice he had already made without realizing it.

Reflection

Sometimes life doesn't ask for permission before it changes direction. It simply places you at a crossroads—between who you were, who you are expected to be, and who you might become if you finally choose yourself.

Chapter 57

Arav sat on the edge of the bed, elbows resting on his knees, his mind drifting—against his will—back to his mother. Her laughter echoed faintly in his memory, warm and familiar. She had always known when something troubled him, even when he tried to hide it. One look, one quiet question, and he would unravel.

But those memories no longer brought comfort alone.

They were now shadowed by unease.

Her death had been labeled an accident. Everyone had accepted it—quickly, neatly. Yet something about it had never settled inside him. The silence that followed her passing felt too clean. Too controlled.

He leaned forward and pulled open the drawer of her nightstand.

Inside were stacks of folded papers—old grocery lists, reminders scribbled in her careful handwriting, notes meant for the house staff. Ordinary things. Domestic. Harmless.

Then he saw it.

A single letter, tucked beneath the others.

It was addressed to his father.

The handwriting was unmistakably his mother's—but shakier than he remembered, the strokes uneven, as if written in haste or fear. Aarav's pulse quickened as he unfolded it.

Rajesh,

I know what you've done.

You think I don't, but I do.

I've kept quiet for years, but I can't anymore.

If you don't tell him the truth, I will.

The letter ended there.

The final line smeared, the ink distorted—as if the pen had been dragged away mid-sentence.

Aarav stared at the page, his breath shallow.

What truth?

And who was him?

His thoughts spiraled, each question spawning another. His father's face surfaced in his mind—controlled, unreadable, always five steps ahead. For the first time, Aarav felt something close to fear—not of losing his father's approval, but of discovering who his father truly was.

He couldn't focus on anything else after that.

The letter burned in his thoughts, its weight unbearable. He needed to speak to someone—someone he trusted. The realization that the list was painfully short made his chest tighten.

That evening, he called Ruchika.

"Can we meet?" he asked, unable to keep the tension from his voice.

"Of course," she replied immediately. "Where?"

They met at a small café on the outskirts of the city, quiet and discreet—far from the circles that surrounded his family. Aarav chose a corner table, away from windows and noise. As soon as Ruchika sat down, he slid the letter across the table.

She read it in silence, her expression growing more serious with every line.

"This... this is from your mother?" she asked softly, looking up.

He nodded. "I found it in her room last night. I don't know what it means—but I can't shake the feeling that it's connected to her death."

Ruchika hesitated. "Aarav... are you sure you want to go down this road?" Her voice was gentle but cautious. "What if it leads to something you're not ready to face?"

"I have to," he said without hesitation. "I can't ignore this. Not when there's a chance that my father—"

His voice faltered. He couldn't finish the sentence.

Ruchika reached across the table, covering his hand with hers. "Whatever you find," she said quietly, "you won't have to face it alone. I'm here."

Her words steadied him—but they didn't ease the knot tightening in his stomach.

Over the next few days, Aarav began investigating quietly. He reviewed police reports. He spoke to members of the house staff who had been present that day. He even tracked down the doctor who had officially pronounced his mother dead.

Each conversation left him more unsettled than the last.

The timeline didn't align. Details were vague. Answers were rehearsed. It felt as though everyone was protecting something—or someone.

Ruchika became his anchor during that time. She listened without judgment, helped organize documents, asked the questions he was too afraid to voice aloud. When his resolve wavered, she reminded him why he had started.

One evening, as they sat in her apartment surrounded by old photographs and papers spread across the floor, Ruchika finally spoke the thought they had both been avoiding.

"Aarav," she said carefully, "have you considered the possibility that your father knows more than he's telling you?"

The room went silent.

Aarav didn't answer—but the look in his eyes said everything.

Reflection

Sometimes the truth doesn't arrive all at once—it seeps in slowly, through unanswered questions and uneasy silences, until you realize the person you trusted most may be standing between you and the truth itself.

Chapter 58

He looked at her sharply. "You think he's involved?"

"I don't know," Ruchika said carefully. "But he's a powerful man. And powerful people often have secrets."

Aarav's jaw tightened. "If he's hiding something about my mother's death, I'll find out. No matter what it takes."

That night, Aarav returned home late, his thoughts racing. The mansion was quiet in a way that felt deliberate, every hallway heavy with unspoken tension. He found his father in the study, bent over a stack of financial reports, reading glasses perched low on his nose.

"We need to talk," Aarav said, his voice flat.

Rajesh glanced up. "Can it wait? I'm in the middle of something."

"No," Aarav said, stepping closer. He pulled the letter from his pocket and placed it on the desk. "Do you recognize this?"

Rajesh froze.

He picked up the letter slowly, his expression darkening as he read. "Where did you find this?" he asked.

"In Mom's room," Aarav replied. "What does it mean? What truth was she talking about?"

Rajesh set the letter down, his hand trembling just enough to give him away. "You shouldn't have found this," he said quietly.

"That's not an answer," Aarav snapped. "What are you hiding?"

Rajesh stood, his presence suddenly imposing. "Leave it alone, Aarav. Some things are better left in the past."

"I deserve the truth," Aarav said, his voice rising. "She was my mother."

Rajesh's eyes flashed. "Your mother was sick," he said sharply. "She wasn't thinking clearly. That letter means nothing."

But Aarav didn't believe him.

There was something in his father's tone—too defensive, too controlled—that confirmed what Aarav had feared. This wasn't the whole truth.

Reflection

Sometimes denial speaks louder than confession.

Chapter 59

The days after the confrontation were heavy with tension. The house felt colder, quieter. Rajesh withdrew further into his work, burying himself in meetings and phone calls, while Aarav avoided him entirely. It became a silent war, fought with distance and restraint.

Through it all, Ruchika became Aarav's anchor.

She began showing up under the excuse of work—brief meetings that lingered longer than necessary. She always brought something small with her: coffee, a book she thought he'd like, or sometimes just herself. She never asked too many questions. She didn't push. She stayed.

One evening, as Aarav paced the terrace overlooking the city, Ruchika stepped outside holding two mugs of chai.

"Here," she said, offering him one. "You look like you could use a pause."

He took it, their fingers brushing briefly. "I haven't been sleeping much."

"I can tell," she said gently. "Your eyes give it away."

They stood side by side, the city glowing beneath them. The silence wasn't uncomfortable. It was steady.

"Sometimes I feel like I'm drowning," Aarav said finally. "Between my father, the business, and now this... I don't know how much more I can hold."

Ruchika turned toward him. "You don't have to hold it alone."

Something in her voice broke through his defenses. He reached for her hand. "Thank you," he said quietly. "For staying."

She didn't pull away. She squeezed his hand once. "Always."

Aarav had just begun to let her in—carefully, cautiously—when the universe shifted again.

The next afternoon, while reviewing contracts in his office, his phone buzzed on the desk.

He glanced down.

And his breath caught.

It was a message from Aimee.

"Aarav, I need your help. Please. I'm in trouble."

The message was short. Rushed. Desperate.

A cold chill ran through Aarav as he read it again. And again.

He didn't hesitate. He called her immediately.

It rang once. Twice. Then went to voicemail.

"Aimee," he said, his voice tight. "Where are you? What's going on? Call me back. Please."

He sent another message. Then another.

Nothing.

Panic crept in slowly, tightening around his chest as questions collided in his mind. What kind of trouble was she in? Why had she reached out now—after months of silence?

When Ruchika walked into his office later that afternoon, she found him pacing, his phone clenched in his hand like an anchor.

"Aarav," she said gently. "What's wrong?"

He stopped, hesitating. "I got a message from someone I used to know. She's in trouble."

Ruchika frowned. "Who?"

"Aimee," he said quietly.

Something shifted in her expression, but she said nothing, sensing the weight behind his voice.

"She won't answer," he continued. "I don't know where she is. She just... disappeared."

"Do you think she's okay?" Ruchika asked.

"I don't know," he admitted. "But I can't ignore this."

She studied him for a moment. "Then don't," she said softly. "Just don't lose yourself trying to save someone else."

He exhaled slowly, guilt and gratitude tangled together. "I don't know how to stop thinking about her."

Ruchika rested a hand on his shoulder, grounding him. "Then let's figure it out together."

Chapter 60

Aimee sat alone in a small, dimly lit room, her back pressed against the wall as she stared through a narrow window. Outside, Mumbai pulsed with life—horns blaring, voices rising, the city alive in every direction. Inside, she felt invisible.

She was exhausted. Her hands trembled as she wrapped her arms around herself, trying to keep the fear from spilling over.

She hadn't planned to contact Aarav.

But desperation had made the decision for her.

Now regret followed close behind.

What if he came looking for her? What if she pulled him into something he couldn't escape? She couldn't bear the thought of hurting him again.

Footsteps echoed in the hallway outside her door.

Aimee froze.

She drew the curtains tighter and pressed herself flat against the wall, her breath shallow, her heart pounding so loudly she was sure it could be heard. The footsteps passed. But the fear stayed.

She was running out of places to hide.

Back in his world, Aarav couldn't shake the sense that something was deeply wrong. He combed through old contacts, scrolled through messages, searched for any trace of where Aimee might be. The idea of hiring a private investigator crossed his mind—but instinct held him back.

This felt personal.

Ruchika noticed the change immediately. He was distracted, restless, his thoughts always elsewhere. She tried not to let jealousy take root, reminding herself that concern didn't always mean love—but the ache lingered anyway.

One evening, as they sat quietly in his living room, she finally spoke.

"I know you're worried about her," she said. "But you can't destroy yourself in the process."

He looked at her, torn. "She asked me for help. What kind of person would I be if I ignored that?"

"You wouldn't," she said calmly. "But you also don't have to carry this alone."

He nodded, rubbing his temples. "I just wish I knew where she was."

Aimee moved through the streets of Mumbai like a shadow, her hood pulled low, her steps quick and deliberate. She slipped into a small café and took a seat in the corner, her eyes scanning the room.

Every sound felt too loud. Every glance felt suspicious.

The waiter set a cup of chai in front of her. She wrapped her hands around it, clinging to the warmth, forcing herself to breathe.

She had come to Mumbai for a reason. She couldn't lose focus now.

But as the hours passed and the city outside darkened, her resolve began to crack. She missed the simplicity of her old life. The safety of familiarity.

She missed Aarav.

She pulled out her phone and stared at the message she had sent him. Part of her wished he would appear—steady, certain, protective—like he always used to.

But she knew better.

Nothing was simple anymore.

Aimee stood, left a few bills on the table, and slipped back into the night, disappearing once again into the endless movement of the city.

Reflection

Sometimes the past doesn't come back to be remembered—it comes back because it still needs to be answered.

Chapter 61

The streets of Bandra were alive with their usual chaos—auto rickshaws honking, vendors calling out, the scent of freshly fried vada pav mixing with the salty breeze from the sea. Aarav stepped out of his meeting, his thoughts still tangled in Ruchika's words from earlier that morning. Life in Mumbai had become an endless grind, and yet, strangely, the disorder calmed him.

Then, through the noise and movement, he saw her.

Aimee.

She stood across the street, her head lowered, her posture fragile, as if the city itself might swallow her whole. Aarav froze. His heart pounded as disbelief washed over him. For a split second, he wondered if exhaustion was playing tricks on him.

She wore a loose kurta—nothing like the polished outfits she used to wear in New York—and her hair was pulled back hastily, strands escaping around her face.

Before he could call out, a speeding auto rickshaw shot past. Aimee stumbled.

Aarav reacted without thinking, weaving through traffic, adrenaline surging through him.

"Aimee!" he called, his voice cracking.

She looked up.

The moment their eyes met, her composure shattered. She took an unsteady step forward and collapsed into his arms. Aarav caught her just in time, holding her as her body shook with sobs.

"I... I didn't know where else to go," she whispered against his chest. "I didn't think I'd ever see you again, Aarav."

He held her, steady and firm, his mind spinning. Months of absence. Silence. And now she was here—raw, broken in a way he had never seen before.

"It's okay," he murmured softly.

But even as she trembled in his arms, Aarav noticed something that startled him.

He wasn't unraveling.

He was concerned. Deeply. But the old instinct—to fix her, to disappear inside her pain—was gone. He felt present, grounded. Changed.

That realization unsettled him more than the reunion itself.

He guided her to a nearby café and chose a quiet corner table. Aimee wrapped both hands around a glass of water, her fingers shaking. Aarav watched her patiently, waiting.

"I'm sorry," she said at last, her voice barely audible. "For reaching out like that. For disappearing. For everything."

"What happened, Aimee?" he asked calmly. "Why are you here?"

She hesitated, staring at her hands. "I ran away," she said finally. "From New York. From my job. From... Logan."

The name landed heavily, but Aarav didn't react. He simply nodded.

"After we broke up," she continued, "I felt empty. Like I'd destroyed everything with you and didn't deserve to feel whole again. Logan was there. He was patient. Kind. He never made me feel like I had to defend myself."

Aarav's jaw tightened, but he stayed silent.

"It started as friendship," she said. "Dance competitions. Long conversations. Late nights. And then one day, he kissed me, and everything shifted."

She paused, swallowing.

"What changed everything," she added softly, "was Paris."

Aarav looked up.

"He planned a trip—not as some romantic escape, but because he knew it was my hometown. He remembered how much I missed it."

Her fingers traced the rim of the glass.

"When he gave me the tickets, he said, 'If Paris is your soul, I want to know every corner of it.'"

Her voice wavered.

Being back in Paris had felt unreal. It wasn't just the city—it was the parts of herself she thought she'd lost. Logan followed her through it all, quietly, attentively.

They walked along the Seine while she told him stories about her mother. She took him to her favorite boulangerie, where they shared a pain au chocolat. In the Marais, she showed him the small bookstore she used to escape into as a child.

"He listened," she whispered. "Like every memory mattered. Like I mattered."

She finally looked up at Aarav, her eyes shining with unshed tears.

"He never asked me to be anything other than myself."

Reflection

What unsettled him most was not her return—but the realization that love no longer asked him to disappear inside it.

Chapter 62

One evening, Logan surprised her again—this time with a picnic beneath the Eiffel Tower. As the lights shimmered against the Parisian night sky, he pulled out a small sketchbook.

"I didn't even know he could draw," Aimee said quietly. "But he'd been sketching me. Little moments—from the bakery, the bookstore, the walks along the river. He said he wanted to capture the parts of me I didn't see in myself."

That night, sitting beneath the glowing monument, Logan took her hand.

"You're home, Aimee," he told her softly. "And I want to be part of that home, if you'll let me."

As she spoke, Aimee's voice faltered. Tears welled in her eyes.

"He was everything I thought I wanted," she said. "Everything I thought I needed."

Aarav felt his chest tighten, but he didn't interrupt.

"But then..." Her voice trailed off. She looked down at her hands.

"What happened?" Aarav asked, quietly.

She shook her head, fingers tightening around the edge of the table. "I don't know if it was me, or him, or just... life. But something changed when we went back to New York. Paris faded. Reality came back."

She took a breath, steadying herself.

"I started noticing things I hadn't before. How he didn't really understand why my independence mattered so much. How he assumed I'd eventually rearrange my life to fit into his."

Her voice grew softer. "And when I pulled back—like I always do—he didn't react the way you did. He didn't cling. He didn't question. He just... withdrew."

The silence between them felt heavy.

"And then," she said, barely above a whisper, "it ended."

Aarav leaned forward. "How?"

But Aimee didn't answer. She turned toward the window, watching the street beyond the glass.

For a long moment, neither of them spoke. The café noises blurred into the background.

Finally, she looked back at him, her eyes full of regret.

"I'm sorry," she said. "For hurting you. For not knowing how to stay."

Aarav studied her face. He wanted to say something comforting, something wise—but nothing felt honest enough.

Instead, he reached across the table and took her hand.

"You don't have to explain everything tonight," he said.

But even as he said it, he knew this wasn't finished. Aimee hadn't come to Mumbai by accident. And Logan—Paris—New York—none of it explained the fear he still saw behind her eyes.

There was more she wasn't telling him.

"I'm just going to grab something," Logan said casually as he slipped on his jacket.

Aimee raised an eyebrow. "At this hour? What do you need?"

"Just some fresh air," he replied with an easy smile. "I'll be back in no time."

Something about his tone unsettled her, but she pushed the feeling aside. Logan had always been attentive, reassuring. He leaned in, kissed her forehead, and disappeared into the Parisian night.

Chapter 63

Minutes stretched into an hour.

Aimee stood by the window of their Airbnb, staring down at the quiet street. Just as she reached for her phone, she saw him approaching. Her stomach tightened.

Logan stumbled slightly as he walked, his steps uneven. When he entered the room, his eyes—usually clear and warm—looked distant, unfocused.

"Logan," she said softly. "Are you... drunk?"

He laughed, the sound hollow. "Not exactly," he muttered, dropping onto the couch.

Aimee moved closer, her unease turning into fear. "What's going on? What did you take?"

"Relax," he said, waving her off. "Just something to take the edge off."

Her chest tightened. "Are you on drugs?"

He didn't answer.

That silence shattered something in her.

"I trusted you," she said, her voice shaking. "You brought me here—my home—and this is what you do?"

Logan straightened, irritation flashing across his face. "You're making it a bigger deal than it is. Everyone does it."

"Everyone?" she snapped. "You can barely sit upright."

"Calm down," he slurred, reaching for her hand.

She pulled away. "Don't tell me to calm down."

Tears streamed down her face, anger and disbelief colliding inside her. "You said you wanted to be part of my life. But this—this isn't safety. This isn't honesty."

Despite everything, she couldn't leave him like this. She guided him to the bedroom, helped him lie down, ignored his slurred apologies.

She sat beside him as he drifted into an uneasy sleep.

That night, Aimee didn't rest.

She watched him breathe, listened to him stir, and felt something shift inside her—quietly, irrevocably. The image she had built of Logan no longer matched the man lying beside her.

By morning, he was apologetic. Remorseful. Convincing.

She told herself it was a mistake. A single lapse. She wanted to believe him because believing felt easier than starting over.

For a while, things seemed fine.

Logan was attentive again. Warm. Present. He made her feel wanted, cherished. Aimee threw herself into work during the day, grateful for the distraction, and in the evenings he was there—meals planned, conversations light, everything smooth on the surface.

But gradually, without announcement, small things began to change.

One evening, after a particularly grueling day at work, Aimee came home exhausted, her nerves frayed and her patience thin. Logan greeted her with his usual easy smile, but there was something else there too—an energy she couldn't quite place.

"You look wrecked," he said, pulling her into an embrace. "Long day?"

"You have no idea," she muttered, dropping her bag by the door.

"I've got something that might help," Logan said lightly, guiding her toward the couch.

She raised an eyebrow. "Wine? Chocolate? Please tell me it's chocolate."

"Better," he said, reaching into his pocket.

When he opened his hand, Aimee froze.

A small bag. White powder.

"Logan... what is that?" Her voice was quiet, cautious.

He chuckled softly, as if she were being adorable. "Relax. It's nothing intense. Just something to help you unwind. You trust me, don't you?"

Her stomach tightened. Every instinct told her to step back, to say no. But Logan's tone was calm, reassuring—practiced.

"I don't know," she said slowly. "That's not really—"

"Aimee," he interrupted gently, brushing his thumb along her knuckles. "You've been under so much pressure. This isn't about getting wild. It's just about letting go. Just for tonight."

He smiled at her—the same smile that had once made her feel protected, chosen.

Against her better judgment, she nodded.

The first time felt exactly as he promised. Warm. Weightless. The tension she carried everywhere loosened its grip. Her laughter came easier, her thoughts softened, and Logan stayed close—his hand in hers, his voice low and affectionate, telling her how beautiful she was, how much he loved seeing her relaxed.

The next morning, guilt settled in.

She told herself it had been a mistake. A line crossed once and never again.

Logan didn't argue. He didn't lecture. He simply kissed her forehead and said, "Don't punish yourself. You're allowed to breathe sometimes."

Her resolve weakened.

What started as something occasional slowly threaded itself into their routine. Logan never pushed outright. He just knew when to suggest it—after a bad day, a difficult meeting, a moment when she looked overwhelmed.

"This is our thing," he'd say. "Just us."

At first, Aimee didn't notice the shift. She was still showing up to work, still answering emails, still moving through her days. But gradually, mornings became heavier. Her focus dulled. Deadlines slipped.

Friends noticed before she did.

"You okay?" they'd ask, glancing at the shadows under her eyes.

"I'm fine," she'd reply, smiling too quickly. "Just tired."

Logan noticed everything.

And he always had a solution.

Reflection

It didn't happen all at once.
That was the most dangerous part.

Chapter 64

Aimee didn't feel like she was losing herself—only that she was borrowing relief, trusting love, choosing comfort. By the time she sensed something was wrong, the choice no longer felt like hers alone.

And yet, every night, Aimee found herself back in Logan's arms—back inside that familiar haze where consequences softened and doubt grew quiet.

Logan's hold on her wasn't just chemical. It was emotional, deliberate.

"I don't know what I'd do without you," he would say, his voice low and earnest, as if confessing something sacred. "You're the only person who really sees me."

Those words settled heavily in her chest. She began to feel responsible not just for his happiness, but for his survival. Leaving didn't feel like freedom anymore—it felt like abandonment.

One night, as they lay tangled together, he said it plainly.

"You're all I have, Aimee. Don't ever leave me."

She didn't answer. She just stared at the ceiling, a quiet unease spreading through her ribs.

The collapse came suddenly.

She arrived home late one evening, exhausted, her head throbbing. Logan was already there—pacing, unfocused, his eyes glassy in a way she recognized immediately.

"What happened?" she asked carefully.

"Nothing," he muttered, refusing to meet her gaze.

Her chest tightened. "Logan. What did you take?"

He laughed, sharp and defensive. "Why do you care now?"

"Because I love you," she said, her voice cracking. "And I'm scared. This isn't okay anymore."

His expression hardened. "You don't get to act innocent. You were right here with me, remember?"

The words hit harder than any accusation. She had no defense—only guilt.

After that night, Aimee tried to pull back. She stayed later at work. Ignored his suggestions. Told herself she needed space.

Logan noticed immediately.

"Don't do this," he pleaded. "I need you."

And every time, she stayed.

But the cost was steep. Her work slipped. Friends stopped calling. Mornings felt heavier than nights. She barely recognized herself.

She knew she had to leave.

She just didn't know how.

The moment of clarity came behind the wheel.

Driving home after another blurred evening, her hands clenched around the steering wheel as the city lights smeared into color and motion. A figure stepped into the road.

She swerved.

The car skidded to a violent stop, heart hammering as she sat frozen, breath shallow, hands shaking.

For a long moment, she couldn't move.

Then she started crying.

That was it.

Not because she was afraid of dying—but because she was afraid of continuing to live like this.

That was the night Aimee left New York.

Left Logan.

Left everything she had been losing herself to.

Reflection

Aimee didn't leave because she was strong.
She left because staying meant disappearing completely.

Chapter 65

Aarav sat silently across from her as she finished, wiping tears from her face, her body trembling under the weight of everything she had just confessed.

He didn't interrupt. Didn't rush to fix it.

But one thing was unmistakably clear.

She couldn't be alone.

"Let's get you somewhere safe," he said at last, his voice quieter than it had been in years.

"Safe?" she whispered.

"My place," Aarav said gently, but firmly. "You don't have to figure everything out tonight. Just... let me help you stand again."

And for the first time in a long while, Aimee didn't argue.

Aimee opened her mouth to protest but stopped when she saw the resolve in Aarav's eyes. She didn't have the strength to argue—and, more than that, she didn't want to be alone. For the first time in months, a fragile sense of relief settled in her chest. Someone was staying. Not out of obligation—but choice.

The drive back to Aarav's house was quiet. The city lights blurred past as Aimee sat curled into the passenger seat, her arms folded tightly around herself. Aarav glanced at her once, then again. The woman beside him felt unfamiliar—smaller, subdued, hollowed out by something he could only guess at. The Aimee he had loved—quick-witted, alive, unapologetically herself—felt distant, almost unreal.

When they arrived, Aarav shut off the engine and exhaled slowly.

"Aimee," he said, turning toward her, "you can stay here as long as you need. But I need you to understand something—this won't be simple. My family—"

"Your family?" she echoed softly.

"Yes," he said, rubbing the back of his neck. "They're traditional. They may not understand why you're here. But that's not your concern. I'll handle it."

She nodded, too tired to ask questions she didn't have the energy to face. Right now, safety mattered more than explanations.

Later that evening, Aarav found Ruchika in the living room, scrolling through her phone. She looked up when he entered, her smile fading as soon as she saw his expression.

"What's wrong?" she asked.

He didn't sit. "Aimee is staying here."

Ruchika blinked. "Excuse me?"

"She's going through something serious. She doesn't have anywhere else to go."

Silence stretched between them.

"This is your ex," Ruchika said carefully. "The woman who walked away from you. And now she's living under the same roof?"

"She's not the same person," Aarav replied. "She needs help. I'm not turning my back on her."

"And where does that leave me?" Ruchika asked, her voice tight. "Do I even matter right now?"

"This isn't about us," Aarav said. "It's about doing the right thing."

Ruchika's composure cracked. "Everything with you becomes about her eventually."

"You're here because my father wants you here," Aarav said, the truth spilling out before he could stop it.

Her breath caught. "Say that again."

He swallowed. "Ruchika, I respect you. I care about you. But I won't pretend this is love."

Her eyes shone, but her voice was steady. "Fine. Then don't expect me to stay and watch you unravel your life."

She walked away without looking back.

Chapter 66

Aimee's first days in Aarav's home passed in quiet discomfort. Dev was polite but reserved, his eyes filled with unanswered questions. The staff spoke in lowered voices, glancing at her when they thought she wasn't looking.

Ruchika barely acknowledged her.

The distance was unmistakable.

That night, Aimee sat on the edge of the guest bed, staring at the unfamiliar room—the heavy furniture, the intricate artwork, the scent of incense lingering in the air. Nothing about it felt like hers. She felt like a guest who had overstayed her welcome before even unpacking.

A soft knock broke the silence.

Aarav stepped inside. "How are you holding up?"

She hesitated, then spoke honestly. "I feel like I don't belong anywhere."

He nodded, as if he already knew. "You don't have to figure anything out tonight."

Reflection

Sometimes safety doesn't feel warm or familiar.

Sometimes it feels like borrowed space—quiet, uncertain, and necessary for survival.

"You'll get used to it," Aarav said, sitting beside her. "It's different, I know. But you're safe here."

Aimee nodded, blinking rapidly as tears gathered. "Thank you, Aarav. For everything."

He hesitated, then placed a gentle hand on her shoulder—careful, deliberate. "Get some rest. We'll figure things out tomorrow."

Aarav arranged for her to see a counselor, and most mornings were spent in therapy, carefully unpacking years of buried trauma. Each session peeled back layers she had survived by ignoring, leaving her lighter and heavier all at once.

The afternoons were harder.

Left alone in the vast house, Aimee wandered from room to room, acutely aware of the unspoken tension that clung to the walls. Every glance felt weighted. Every silence felt loud.

Ruchika's presence was the sharpest.

"You don't belong here," Ruchika said one evening, her voice low and controlled.

Aimee flinched but kept her gaze steady. "I never asked to be here," she replied quietly. "Aarav insisted."

Ruchika let out a humorless laugh. "Of course he did. He always had a weakness for you."

Aimee said nothing. She had learned when silence was safer than defense.

As days turned into weeks, small pockets of relief appeared. Dev, reserved but observant, softened toward her. He asked about New York, about her work, about what she hoped to do next. His kindness was understated, but it mattered.

Chapter 67

Still, Aarav was her constant.

Despite his long hours, he checked in—sometimes with words, sometimes just by sitting beside her. He listened without trying to fix her. He no longer hovered or demanded reassurance.

That change unsettled her.

This Aarav was calmer. Steadier. No longer orbiting her existence.

And part of her—ashamed, frightened—missed the version of him who had once needed her as much as she now needed him.

One evening in the garden, she finally said it.

"You've changed."

Aarav looked at her, thoughtful. "We both have."

Her chest tightened. "I don't know who I am anymore."

"You will," he said evenly. "You're stronger than you realize."

That night, the house fell quiet early. Dev retired. Aarav disappeared into his study. Aimee sat alone near the patio, watching a small diya flicker in the dark.

The flame should have comforted her. Instead, it illuminated how empty she felt.

Therapy helped—but it also left her exposed. At night, when there was nothing to distract her, memories rushed in. New York. The life she abandoned. Logan.

The anger came easily. The guilt followed just as fast.

He had led her here—but she had followed.

The crunch of gravel broke her thoughts. Aarav approached, handing her a glass of water before sitting beside her.

"You okay?" he asked.

"I don't know," she admitted.

He didn't ask for more. He stayed.

Healing did not arrive as relief. It arrived as awareness—and awareness was exhausting.

"You don't have to do this," Aimee said after a long silence.

"Do what?"

"Take care of me. Let me stay here." Her voice wavered. "I know I've... disrupted your life."

Aarav leaned back in his chair and exhaled slowly. "You're not a disruption, Aimee. You needed help. And I'm not going to turn my back on you."

She looked at him then, really looked at him. Her eyes shimmered with unshed tears.

"I don't deserve your kindness."

"That's not for you to decide," Aarav said, his tone firm, final.

Inside the house, Ruchika paced her room, her thoughts spiraling. She had tried to ignore Aimee's presence, tried to convince herself it was temporary, harmless. But the tension refused to ease.

Aarav was spending more time with Aimee. And no matter how carefully he framed it—concern, responsibility, decency—Ruchika felt something slipping through her fingers.

The final crack came the next morning.

At breakfast, she heard it.

Aarav's laughter.

It wasn't loud. It wasn't exaggerated. But it was real. And it was directed at Aimee.

Ruchika froze, the sound cutting through her like a blade.

She waited until Aimee left the table before speaking.

"Can we talk?" Her voice was clipped, controlled.

Aarav set his coffee down. "What's on your mind?"

"This situation with Aimee," Ruchika said, choosing her words carefully. "It's too much. She's living here. You're always with her. And I feel like I'm just... standing in the way."

"You're not in the way," Aarav replied evenly.

"Then what am I?" Her composure cracked. "Because right now, I feel invisible."

Aarav sighed. "Ruchika, I was clear from the start. This isn't about us. Aimee needs help, and I'm not abandoning her."

"And what about me?" she asked sharply. "Do I not need you too?"

His expression hardened. "I'm doing what's right. You're making this about yourself when it's not."

Ruchika let out a bitter laugh. "You're lying to yourself if you think this is just pity. You still care about her."

Aarav didn't answer.

His silence did.

Ruchika grabbed her bag and walked out without another word, leaving him alone at the table.

Chapter 68

Adjusting to life in Aarav's home was harder than Aimee had imagined.

The cultural differences were stark. The house felt formal, structured—every movement observed. The staff were polite but distant, their whispers a constant reminder that she did not belong.

Even meals felt isolating. The food overwhelmed her, and she quietly settled for plain rice and vegetables, not wanting to draw attention.

But the heaviest weight was emotional.

Ruchika's cold glances. The tension she could feel but never address. The knowledge that her presence had shifted something—maybe broken something.

One afternoon, she tried to make tea.

She burned the pot.

Ruchika walked in as Aimee stood frozen, staring at the mess.

"Tea isn't exactly your strength, is it?" Ruchika said lightly.

"I'm trying," Aimee replied, her face flushing.

Ruchika folded her arms. "Why are you here, Aimee? What do you actually want?"

"I don't know," Aimee admitted, her voice trembling. "I just didn't know where else to go."

For a moment, something unreadable crossed Ruchika's face. Then it hardened again.

"You're lucky Aarav still cares enough to do this," she said coolly. "Just don't confuse his kindness for something more."

Aimee said nothing. She couldn't.

Despite his calm exterior, Aarav was unraveling.

The business demanded him. His father watched him closely. Ruchika was slipping away. And Aimee's presence was stirring emotions he believed he had already buried.

Late that night, he found Aimee on the balcony, staring at the city lights.

"Can't sleep?" he asked quietly, sitting beside her.

Kindness often arrives before forgiveness—and that makes it harder to accept.

She shook her head. "It's hard. My mind just... won't stop."

Aarav nodded, leaning against the railing beside her. "It gets better. Slowly."

Aimee studied his face, as if searching for certainty there. "Do you think I'll ever feel normal again?"

"I think you'll find a new normal," Aarav said honestly. "But it takes time. And you have to let yourself heal."

Her eyes filled. "Thank you, Aarav. For everything."

"You don't have to thank me," he replied gently. "Just focus on getting better."

In the days that followed, Aimee began taking small, deliberate steps toward rebuilding herself. She started journaling, filling pages with thoughts she had kept buried for too long. She spent time outside, walking through the garden, letting the sun warm her skin and quiet the constant noise in her head.

Still, the unease lingered.

Despite the progress, she felt untethered—like she was floating, with Aarav as the only thing anchoring her to solid ground.

Aarav remained present, supportive—but distant. He showed up when she needed him, listened without judgment, helped without asking for anything in return. He was no longer the anxious, emotionally dependent man she had once known.

This version of him was steady. Self-contained.

And while Aimee admired that strength, it also reminded her of how fragile she had become.

One evening, as they sat in the living room, she turned to him quietly.

"Do you ever think about the past? About us?"

Aarav held her gaze for a moment. "Sometimes. But I try not to live there. It's not healthy."

She nodded, though her chest tightened.

She missed the way he used to look at her—as if she were his entire world. Now, she wasn't sure what she was to him at all.

Chapter 69

Twilight found Aimee alone on the terrace again.

The Mumbai sky was streaked with burnt orange and dusky pink, beautiful in a way that still felt foreign to her. She sat cross-legged on the concrete ledge, the humid air clinging to her skin. Below, traffic hummed like a restless tide. Up here, the quiet pressed in.

From inside the house, Ruchika's laughter drifted through the open windows—soft, musical, effortless.

Aimee hated how it twisted something inside her.

She hadn't meant to fall back into wanting Aarav. But without warning, her thoughts kept circling him. In the stillness of his home—technically a guest room, though it felt like a shadow of something that once belonged to her—she noticed the details.

The way he walked barefoot when exhausted.

The exact tone of his voice when he ordered tea.

The way his smile never quite reached his eyes anymore when he looked at her.

What had she expected?

That she'd return broken, unraveling—and he would gather her back into himself like before?

No.

That man no longer existed.

And yet, she wanted that comfort. Wanted it so badly her chest ached with the weight of it.

She leaned her head against the railing, swallowing the tightness in her throat.

A shadow shifted near the terrace door.

Aarav.

He stepped out quietly, dressed in a plain white T-shirt and black joggers. His gaze found her slowly, cautiously.

"I figured you'd be up here," he said.

She turned away, brushing at her cheek. "I needed air."

"You didn't eat dinner."

"I wasn't hungry."

He sat beside her—but not close.

There was space between them, intentional and measured, like a boundary he refused to blur.

Aimee's voice cracked. "You've changed."

Aarav didn't answer right away. Then, quietly, "You think so?"

"You're colder now," she said, the words heavy as they fell. "Like you've built this wall around yourself. Like no one can get in."

He let out a short, humorless breath. "That's an interesting observation—coming from you."

Her eyes flashed. "What's that supposed to mean?"

"It means," he said evenly, "you spent months pushing me away. I kept chasing something that didn't want to be held. And now that I've stopped... you think I'm the one who changed?"

Aimee pressed her lips together until she tasted blood. "I didn't realize I'd lose you completely."

Aarav looked out over the city. "You didn't lose me."

He turned back to her.

"You let me go."

The silence that followed was absolute. There was nothing left to defend. They both knew it.

She folded into herself, arms wrapped around her knees. "I don't know who I am anymore," she whispered. "I wake up every day hoping I'll feel like myself again—and I don't. I'm still scared. I'm still addicted."

He tensed.

"Not to drugs," she added quickly. "To the numbness. Everything hurts again."

Her voice broke, and her body followed—small tremors turning into something she couldn't control.

Aarav turned sharply. "Hey—"

He reached for her without thinking, his hand closing around hers.

That was all it took.

She collapsed into sobs—raw, unrestrained, like months of silence tearing free at once. Her breath came in broken gasps, her body shaking as if she might come apart.

Aarav pulled her into his arms.

She didn't resist.

She clung to him like he was the last solid thing she recognized. Her tears soaked into his shirt. He held her—one hand firm at her back, the other steady in her hair—anchoring her without a word.

He didn't promise anything.

He didn't explain.

He just stayed.

When the sobbing finally ebbed into quiet breaths, she pulled away, her face swollen, her eyes rimmed red.

"I never meant for any of this," she said faintly. "I didn't know how far I'd fall."

Aarav studied her for a long moment. "I know."

Her voice dropped to a whisper. "But I miss you."

Something softened in his eyes—only briefly.

"Aimee," he said gently, "I'm not yours to miss anymore."

The words landed hard.

"I'm with Ruchika," he continued, careful, steady. "Maybe it's not what we had. But it's grounded. It doesn't scare me."

Her breath caught. "And I scared you?"

"Yes," he said honestly. "I was always waiting for you to leave."

She swallowed. "I didn't mean to."

"I know," he said again—quiet, resigned.

"But I can be better," she said, reaching for his hand. "I am getting better."

He let her hold it—just for a moment.

Then, gently, he eased his hand free.

She nodded, understanding more in that movement than any explanation could offer.

He stood. "I should go. Ruchika's waiting."

She rose too, arms wrapped tightly around herself. "Of course."

Before leaving, he turned back once.

"You'll be okay," he said.

And for the first time, she believed he meant it—even if he wouldn't be there to see it.

Chapter 70

But neither of them really believed that.

The days that followed were thick with things left unsaid.

Aimee stayed mostly in the guest room, emerging only when necessary, careful not to cross paths with Aarav more than she had to. Still, the house made it impossible to disappear completely. Every time she heard his voice down the hall—lighter, warmer, directed at Ruchika—something inside her cracked just a little more.

She hated herself for it.

She didn't want to be this version of herself—jealous, fragile, reaching for something she had already lost. But every shared laugh, every casual babe from Ruchika's lips, made the walls close in tighter.

One morning, she walked into the kitchen and found Ruchika alone, stirring her coffee.

They exchanged a brief nod. Civil. Distant.

"You should eat something," Ruchika said, still watching the cup.

"I'm not hungry," Aimee replied.

"You haven't been hungry in days."

Aimee didn't respond.

Ruchika exhaled slowly. "Look, I know you and Aarav have history. But he's moved on."

Aimee stiffened. "I'm not here to take him from you."

Ruchika glanced up then, her expression unreadable. "Could've fooled me."

The words landed hard. Aimee opened her mouth—then closed it again. There was nothing she could say that wouldn't sound like an excuse.

That evening, voices drifted through the hallway.

"You didn't need to be so sharp with her," Aarav said.

"I wasn't sharp," Ruchika replied. "I was honest."

"She's still recovering—"

"And what about us, Aarav?" Ruchika interrupted. "Are we pretending her presence doesn't change things?"

Silence followed.

Aimee stepped away from the door, her heart pounding. She hadn't meant to wedge herself between them. But somehow, that was always how it ended.

Aarav buried himself in work—meetings, calls, dinners he barely tasted. Yet every time he passed the guest room, he slowed.

She was a storm he didn't trust himself to walk into again.

Ruchika noticed. The distance. The way his mind drifted. The way he pulled back from her touch. She said nothing—until one evening in the garden, tea cooling between them.

"Is something going on with you and her?" she asked quietly.

Aarav looked up. "What?"

"Don't do that," she said. "I can feel it. Ever since she arrived."

He stared into his cup. "She's struggling. That's all."

Ruchika nodded, thoughtful. Then, softly, "And you still love her."

The question struck deeper than he expected.

He didn't answer right away—because the truth wasn't simple.

"I don't know what I feel anymore," he admitted.

Ruchika held his gaze for a moment, then nodded. "Thank you for not lying."

She stood, leaned down, and kissed his forehead—gentle, almost final.

Then she walked back inside.

Aarav stayed where he was.

And for the first time, he didn't follow.

The next morning began like any other.

But something in the air had shifted.

It wasn't visible—not in the gentle clink of breakfast plates or the distant murmur of the household staff preparing for the day. It lived in subtler places. In the way Aimee lingered near the kitchen a little longer than necessary, hoping—foolishly—to catch a glimpse of Aarav before he left. In the way her eyes dropped the instant she saw him pass through the corridor, dressed sharply in a tailored blazer, his hair still damp from the shower, his phone already pressed to his ear.

He didn't look at her.

Chapter 71

That omission twisted something deep in her stomach.

It wasn't that she expected him to stop. But she remembered how he used to pause, how he would always find her eyes even in passing. Now, he moved through the house with practiced efficiency, as if she were just another piece of furniture he had learned to walk around.

She wasn't sure what hurt more—the silence, or the growing realization that she was no longer the center of his world.

Later that day, Aimee wandered into the library.

The room smelled of old wood and quiet wealth, its shelves immaculate, sunlight pouring in through tall windows that softened the sharpness of the space. She ran her fingers along the spine of a leather-bound novel she had read years ago—back when she and Aarav had still been discovering each other.

A story about two people finding their way back to love.

It felt almost cruel now.

The door creaked open behind her.

She turned too quickly, her pulse betraying her hope.

But it wasn't Aarav.

It was Ruchika.

"Oh—hi," Aimee said, stepping away from the shelf. "I didn't think anyone used this room."

Ruchika offered a polite smile as she entered. "I do sometimes. It's the quietest place in the house."

Silence stretched between them, thick and uncomfortable. Aimee stared at the carpet, unsure where to place herself.

Ruchika reached for a poetry book on the coffee table, flipping it open casually. "You've been here a while now."

"Yes," Aimee replied, fidgeting. "Just until I... figure things out."

Ruchika nodded slowly. "And Aarav—does he know what you're trying to figure out?"

Aimee lifted her head. "He's just helping me."

"I know," Ruchika said calmly. "He told me. He said it was pity. That's all."

Aimee flinched. "Right."

Ruchika studied her for a moment, then asked, almost gently, "You still love him, don't you?"

Aimee opened her mouth—then closed it.

She didn't owe her honesty.

But the truth pressed painfully against her chest, and when she spoke, it came out barely louder than a breath. "I don't know who I am without him."

Ruchika's expression softened—not with triumph, but something closer to sadness.

"That's the saddest thing I've ever heard," she said quietly.

Then she turned and left.

Aimee sank onto the small velvet couch, her body heavy with shame and regret. The room felt too large, too quiet. Ruchika had been right.

Somewhere along the way—between love, loss, and survival—she had misplaced herself entirely.

Reflection

Sometimes heartbreak isn't about losing someone—it's about realizing you handed them the map to your identity and forgot to keep one for yourself. Aimee wasn't grieving Aarav anymore; she was grieving the version of herself that only existed when she was chosen.

Chapter 72

Over the next week, Aimee began shadowing Aarav through his daily routine.

She never said it outright, but she found quiet ways to stay close—waiting near the entryway when she knew he was leaving, offering to help with errands, asking questions about his business even when the terminology went over her head.

And Aarav—for the most part—allowed it.

He let her sit in on vendor meetings. He answered her questions patiently. He never rushed her away.

But he also never lingered.

Never reached for her hand.

Never smiled the way he once had.

The distance was deliberate.

One evening, after a long meeting, they sat stalled in traffic, the city lights blurring against the windshield. The car hummed softly around them, heavy with unspoken things.

Aimee turned toward him. "Do you ever think about us?"

He kept his eyes on the road. "I think about a lot of things."

"That's not an answer."

His fingers tightened slightly on the steering wheel. "Aimee—"

"No," she interrupted, her voice trembling. "Please don't say something kind just to soften the truth. I want to know."

Aarav pulled the car over.

Rain had begun to fall, misting the windshield, dulling the world outside. He turned to face her, exhaustion etched into his features.

"You broke me," he said quietly. "And then I had to rebuild myself. It took everything I had to reach a place where I didn't need you just to survive."

Aimee swallowed hard, her throat tightening.

"And now you're here again," he continued, "looking at me like I'm your oxygen. But I can't be that person anymore. I won't."

Tears slid down her cheeks—silent, uncontested.

"I'm sorry," she whispered. "I never meant to—"

"I know," he said gently. "But apologies don't undo the past. They don't erase the nights I couldn't sleep or the days I spent wondering why I wasn't enough for you."

The silence that followed felt endless.

Aimee turned toward the window, her breath fogging the glass. "I didn't come here to ruin your life."

"I know."

She looked back at him, slowly. "But I still need you. Just not in the way I used to."

Something in her voice—honest, fractured, impossibly human—made his chest tighten.

He reached for her hand and rested his own over it.

Just for a moment.

"We should go home," he said quietly.

And so they did.

That night, after dinner, Aimee couldn't sleep.

She wandered the halls in her pajamas, the old wooden floors creaking beneath her feet. Her chest felt tight, her thoughts restless and tangled. No matter how she tried to quiet them, they kept circling back to the same things—Aarav, the house, the person she used to be.

Eventually, she found herself back on the terrace.

The city glowed below, alive and indifferent, its lights stretching endlessly into the distance. Up here, the air felt cooler, thinner—like she could breathe a little easier.

Footsteps sounded behind her.

Of course.

Aarav stood in the doorway, arms loosely crossed. "You okay?"

She turned, her eyes glassy. "No."

He walked closer, his presence steady, familiar in a way that unsettled her.

"What's wrong?"

"I don't know who I am anymore," she said, shaking her head. "I don't know how to be this version of myself. I wake up every day hoping you'll look at me the way you used to. And when you don't... I feel like I'm disappearing."

A bitter laugh slipped out. "Isn't that pathetic?"

"No," he said quietly. "It's human."

Aimee sank down against the cool terrace wall, pulling her knees to her chest. "I'm scared I'll never get better."

Aarav crouched beside her. "You will."

Her breath caught. "Promise?"

He didn't answer.

Instead, she reached for him—impulsive, unguarded—her fingers clutching the sleeve of his shirt. And then she broke.

The sobs came hard and fast, shaking her whole body as she leaned into him, as if the weight of everything she'd carried would finally pull her under.

Aarav held her.

He didn't speak. Didn't try to fix anything. He just wrapped his arms around her, rocking her gently, one hand smoothing over her hair.

His touch was warm. Steady.

But something in him stayed closed.

When the storm finally passed and her breathing slowed, Aimee pulled back, her eyes red, her voice hollow.

"I wish I could go back," she whispered.

"So do I."

Neither of them said what they meant by it.

Chapter 73

In the days that followed, Aarav watched Aimee more closely.

She tried to appear composed—moving through the house with polite smiles, engaging when spoken to—but the signs were there if you knew how to look. The way her gaze drifted mid-conversation. The stiffness in her posture. The faint tremor in her hands when she thought no one was paying attention.

It unsettled him.

One evening, as they sat across from each other in the living room, Aarav broke the silence.

"Come with you," he said.

Aimee looked up. "Where?"

"Your therapy session."

She stiffened immediately. "You don't have to do that."

"I know," he said. "But I want to."

She hesitated, uncertainty flickering across her face. Letting him see her like that—raw, unfiltered—felt terrifying. But beneath the fear was something else. Relief.

"...Okay," she said finally.

They scheduled the appointment for the following week.

Dr. Meera Joshi.

Aimee's therapist.

For the first time since returning to Mumbai, Aimee felt something shift—not relief exactly, but the faint sense that she wouldn't have to walk through this part alone.

And Aarav, watching her across the room, knew that whatever this was between them now—it was different.

Not a rescue.

Not a reunion.

Something quieter.

More fragile.

And far more complicated.

The therapy center was a modest building tucked between narrow Mumbai streets, its quiet presence almost easy to miss. Inside, the air felt lighter—filtered, calm—like the world outside had been gently muted. Aimee and Aarav arrived a few minutes early, sitting side by side without speaking.

Aimee twisted the hem of her blouse between her fingers, a nervous habit she couldn't seem to stop. Aarav sat upright, eyes fixed straight ahead, his jaw tense. He wasn't sure what he was preparing for, only that whatever came next would change something.

Dr. Meera Joshi greeted them with a warm, measured smile. She was in her late forties, composed without being distant, her presence steady in a way that immediately softened the room.

"Aimee, it's good to see you," she said gently, before turning to Aarav. "And you must be Aarav. Aimee has spoken about you."

Aarav inclined his head. "Thank you for letting me sit in today."

"Of course," Dr. Joshi replied, gesturing toward the chairs. "And Aimee—would you be comfortable if Aarav and I spoke privately for a few minutes after the session?"

Aimee hesitated, her eyes flicking to Aarav, searching his face. He gave her a small nod.

"...Okay," she said quietly.

The session unfolded slowly.

Aimee spoke about New York. About Logan. About how being alone felt unbearable, and how needing someone had become second nature to her. Her voice trembled when she admitted how easily she attached herself to anyone who made her feel safe—even when that safety wasn't real.

Aarav listened in silence, his chest tightening. He hadn't known how deep it went. How much of her pain lived beneath the surface.

When the hour ended, Aimee stepped out to the waiting area, leaving Aarav alone with Dr. Joshi.

She folded her hands calmly. "You care about her," she said. "That much is obvious."

"Yes," Aarav admitted. "But I don't know where support ends and damage begins."

Dr. Joshi considered him for a moment. "Aimee struggles with a deep fear of abandonment. When someone becomes her emotional anchor, she holds on tightly—not out of manipulation, but out of survival."

Aarav swallowed. "So by being there... I might be making it harder for her to stand on her own."

"Not deliberately," Dr. Joshi said. "But without boundaries, yes. Healing doesn't come from replacing one dependency with another. It comes from learning to feel whole without being held together by someone else."

Aarav leaned back, exhaling. "I want to help her. But I can't lose myself again."

"And you shouldn't," Dr. Joshi said firmly. "The healthiest thing you can do—for both of you—is to support her growth without becoming the solution to her pain."

He nodded slowly. "Thank you. I needed to hear that."

When he stepped outside, Aimee was flipping through a magazine she clearly wasn't reading. She looked up the moment she sensed him.

"Ready?" he asked.

She stood. "How did it go?"

He hesitated, then offered a gentle smile. "It helped. We'll talk on the way home."

She nodded, accepting that answer.

Chapter 74

For the first time, Aarav understood that saving someone didn't always mean staying close—and Aimee, though she didn't yet know it, was standing at the edge of learning how to survive without being held.

The drive back home passed in silence—no longer awkward, but heavy. The kind of quiet that held too many thoughts to risk speaking aloud. As they pulled into the driveway, the sky was turning amber, the sun slipping behind the Mehta residence as if retreating from what waited inside.

They barely made it to the steps before Ruchika appeared.

She stood at the entrance, arms crossed tightly against her chest, her expression brittle with restraint already close to shattering.

"Where have you been?" she asked, her eyes moving sharply from Aarav to Aimee.

Aarav exhaled. "Ruchika—let's go inside."

"No." Her voice cracked, louder than she intended. "We'll talk now. You've been distant for days. Distracted. And then I find out you've been going to therapy with her?"

Aimee instinctively stepped back, guilt flooding her. "Ruchika, I—"

"This isn't about you," Ruchika snapped, turning briefly toward Aimee before fixing her gaze back on Aarav. "This is about him not telling me the truth."

Aarav stepped forward, lowering his voice. "You're right. I should have told you. Aimee is struggling, and I wanted to help—but I handled this poorly."

Ruchika's composure finally cracked. "Poorly?" she repeated. "You went to therapy with your ex behind my back. How do you think that feels?"

Aarav didn't argue. "It feels like betrayal," he said quietly. "And I'm sorry."

Her eyes filled, though she blinked hard against the tears. "I don't need apologies, Aarav. I need to know where I stand."

"I care about you," he said. "And I don't want to lose what we're building. But I needed to make sure Aimee was safe."

Ruchika laughed softly, bitterly. "And what about me? Do I matter when she needs you?"

Before Aarav could answer, Aimee spoke—her voice small, steady with effort.

"I shouldn't be here," she said. "And I won't be. I didn't come to take anything from you."

Ruchika looked at her, something conflicted flickering across her face. Then she nodded once. "That's probably for the best."

Aimee didn't wait for more. She slipped past them, retreating to the guest room. When the door closed behind her, she leaned against it, breath shaking. For the first time since arriving, she saw the damage clearly—not just to herself, but to everyone around her.

And she knew what she had to do.

Inside the house, the tension still lingered, but behind the closed door of the bedroom, Aarav and Ruchika finally let it surface. Ruchika broke down first—quiet tears, exhaustion replacing anger. Aarav pulled her into his arms, holding her close, steady.

"I'm here," he murmured. "I won't disappear. I promise."

She clung to him, wanting to believe it.

For the first time, all three of them understood the same truth—healing would not come from closeness alone, but from knowing when to step away.

Ruchika nestled deeper into his embrace, her breathing gradually evening out as sleep claimed her. Aarav remained awake, his mind a restless whirl of thoughts and regrets. He knew his actions had hurt her, and the weight of that realization pressed heavily against his chest. Determined to mend the rift between them, he resolved to be more transparent, more attentive—to do better.

Hours later, the stillness of the night was broken by a sudden dryness in his throat. Careful not to disturb Ruchika, Aarav slipped out of bed and padded quietly toward the kitchen. As he passed the hallway, a faint melody caught his attention. Soft music drifted from behind the closed door of Aimee's room—an unusual sound at such a late hour.

Frowning, Aarav slowed and knocked gently.

"Aimee?" he called softly.

No response.

He knocked again, a little louder. "Aimee, are you awake?"

Still nothing.

Unease settled in his chest. Aimee had been making progress, or so he thought, but the late-night music and her silence unsettled him. His knocks grew firmer, echoing through the quiet house.

After a long pause, the door finally creaked open.

Aimee stood there, and alarm shot through him instantly. Her eyes were bloodshot, pupils dilated, cheeks flushed. A familiar scent hung in the air, confirming what he already feared.

"Aimee," he said, disbelief and disappointment bleeding into his voice, "you're high again?"

She swayed slightly, a lazy smile tugging at her lips. "Relax, Aarav. It's just a little something to take the edge off."

His jaw tightened, anger rising despite his effort to stay calm. "How did you even get this? I thought we agreed you were done with all of this."

Aimee rolled her eyes, leaning against the doorframe for support. "Agreed? You mean you decided for me. I'm an adult, Aarav. I can make my own choices."

His hands curled into fists at his sides. "Choices? Aimee, this isn't just about you. You're living under our roof. Ruchika and I have been trying to help you, and this is how you repay us?"

She laughed—a hollow, brittle sound. "Help me? By treating me like a child? By constantly reminding me of my failures?"

Aarav stepped closer, searching her face for even a trace of remorse. "We care about you, Aimee. But you can't keep doing this to yourself."

Her expression faltered. For a moment, the defiance slipped, revealing something raw beneath it. "I don't know how else to cope," she admitted quietly.

The confession softened his anger, replacing it with concern. He reached out, resting a careful hand on her shoulder. "There are better ways. Healthier ways. Let us help you find them."

She looked up at him, tears pooling in her eyes. "I'm scared, Aarav. Scared of facing everything sober."

Chapter 75

He nodded slowly. "I know. But numbing yourself isn't the answer."

The air between them grew heavy, charged with everything they hadn't said. Without realizing how close they'd become, they stood just inches apart, breath mingling, tension tightening like a wire.

Then, impulsively, their lips met.

The kiss was intense—confused, desperate, born of suppressed emotion and blurred boundaries. But almost immediately, reality crashed down on him.

Aarav pulled away sharply, guilt flashing across his face. "This is wrong," he muttered, more to himself than to her. "I shouldn't have... We shouldn't have."

Aimee touched her lips, confusion and longing battling in her eyes. "Aarav..."

He stepped back, creating distance. "I need to go," he said, his voice strained. Without waiting for a response, he turned and walked away, each step heavier than the last.

Back in his bedroom, Aarav slipped beneath the covers beside Ruchika. She stirred slightly, murmuring in her sleep, unaware. Lying there in the darkness, the weight of his actions pressed down on him, making it difficult to breathe.

Sleep refused to come. Guilt sat heavy in his chest, sharper than fear, heavier than desire. He stared into the dark, aware that he had crossed a line he had sworn to protect—not just for Ruchika, but for himself. Helping Aimee had begun as compassion, but somewhere along the way, care had blurred into confusion, and boundaries into weakness.

What unsettled him most wasn't the kiss itself—it was how easily it had happened.

Aarav realized then that love, once broken, didn't disappear. It changed shape. It lingered in reflexes, in old instincts, in moments of vulnerability. And if he wasn't careful, it would cost him everything he was trying to build.

By morning, choices would have to be made.

And this time, there would be no room for mistakes.

What frightened Aarav wasn't desire—it was how easily old patterns resurfaced under pressure. He had believed distance meant healing, that time alone had made him immune to the past. But the moment revealed a harder truth: growth wasn't the absence of feeling, it was the discipline to act differently despite it. Compassion without boundaries had put him in a position he never intended to be in, and now he had to face the cost. If he wanted a future built on clarity instead of chaos, he would have to choose responsibility over instinct—and accept that caring for someone did not mean rescuing them.

Aarav's mind raced as he lay in bed, the darkness of the room mirroring the turmoil inside him. The kiss with Aimee had been brief but intense—an unexpected spark that ignited emotions he hadn't prepared for. Guilt settled deep in his chest, each heartbeat echoing the same relentless question: How could I let this happen?

Beside him, Ruchika stirred softly, her presence a quiet reminder of the commitment he had just endangered. He turned toward her, the pale glow of moonlight tracing gentle shadows across her peaceful face. The contrast between her calm and his unrest made it hard to breathe, as though the weight of his actions had pressed the air from his lungs.

Sleep refused to come. His thoughts drifted backward, replaying moments with Aimee that now carried a different meaning. Their friendship had always been close, but somewhere along the way, the lines had blurred—especially as he stood by her through her most fragile moments. He wondered if he had been naïve to believe their bond could remain uncomplicated.

Chapter 76

The next morning arrived wrapped in an uneasy silence. Aarav found Aimee in the kitchen, cradling a cup of coffee, her gaze fixed firmly away from his. The air between them felt dense, charged with everything neither of them wanted to say.

"Aimee," he began carefully, "about last night—"

"It was a mistake," she cut in, lifting her eyes to meet his. Regret flickered across her face.

He nodded, both relieved and quietly wounded by her certainty. "We need to set boundaries. For both our sakes."

She exhaled, pushing a hand through her hair. "I know. I've been leaning on you too much. You've just... been my anchor through all of this."

Her honesty tightened something in his chest. "I care about you, Aimee," he said gently. "But we can't let our closeness jeopardize the relationships we have with others."

She nodded slowly, absorbing his words. "Maybe it's time I look for more support. I can't rely on you alone."

"That might be best," he agreed, though the admission tasted bitter.

Days passed, and the incident remained unspoken. Aimee began attending therapy more regularly, gradually reclaiming pieces of herself. Aarav, in turn, focused on repairing the quiet fractures in his relationship with Ruchika—who remained unaware of how close he had come to crossing a line he couldn't erase.

One evening, as he and Ruchika prepared dinner together, she paused and set the knife down. "Is everything okay?" she asked, concern softening her voice.

He hesitated, the impulse to confess wrestling with the fear of what honesty might cost. "Why do you ask?"

"You've seemed distant. Distracted."

Aarav drew a slow breath. "There's been a lot on my mind. Work, family... Aimee."

Ruchika studied him closely. "Is she all right?"

"She's struggling," he admitted. "I've been trying to help. But I think I may have gotten too involved."

She held his gaze for a moment before speaking. "I trust you, Aarav. Just remember—you're not responsible for fixing everyone."

Her reassurance only deepened the guilt he carried. He nodded, forcing a small smile. "You're right. I'll be more mindful."

As weeks went by, the household settled into a fragile rhythm. Aimee grew steadier, therapy giving her a foothold again. Aarav and Ruchika worked deliberately at strengthening their bond, choosing communication over avoidance, presence over assumption.

And yet, in the quiet hours—when shadows stretched long and the world softened into stillness—Aarav couldn't escape the memory of that night. The taste of forbidden closeness lingered, a reminder of how easily boundaries could falter, and how some lines, once crossed, never truly faded.

Reflection

Sometimes the most dangerous moments are not born from intention, but from vulnerability—when care quietly turns into dependence, and closeness slips past the edges of restraint. What Aarav carried was not just guilt, but the realization that even good intentions require boundaries, and that accountability begins not in confession, but in choice.

Chapter 77

Aarav lay in bed, the darkness pressing in around him, mirroring the turmoil within. The kiss with Aimee replayed relentlessly in his mind—a moment of weakness that now felt like a widening chasm between him and Ruchika. He turned toward Ruchika, watching the gentle rise and fall of her chest as she slept, peaceful and unaware of the storm he carried beside her.

Sleep refused to come. Every time he closed his eyes, Aimee's face surfaced, the warmth of her lips lingering like a memory he couldn't scrub away. Guilt settled deep within him, sharp and unrelenting. He had crossed a line—one he couldn't erase, no matter how much he wished otherwise.

In the days that followed, Aarav avoided Aimee. He didn't know what to say or how to face her without reopening something fragile and dangerous. He filled his time with small, mindless tasks, hoping distraction might dull the weight of his actions. But the silence between them was louder than any confrontation.

Ruchika noticed the shift almost immediately.

"Is everything okay?" she asked one evening, concern etched across her face.

Aarav forced a smile. "Just tired," he said, avoiding her eyes.

Later that day, Aimee found him.

"We need to talk," she said softly.

They sat in the living room, the air heavy with everything neither of them wanted to name.

"I'm sorry," Aarav began. "I shouldn't have let that happen."

Aimee nodded, tears gathering in her eyes. "I was vulnerable. I leaned on you in ways I shouldn't have. It won't happen again."

They agreed to set boundaries—to focus on healing, to move forward carefully. But even as the words were spoken, Aarav knew the damage had already been done. Too much history remained unresolved. Too many feelings still lingered beneath the surface. The path ahead felt uncertain, risky, and fragile.

Ruchika, sensing the growing distance, began spending as much time with Aarav as she could. One evening, she surprised him entirely.

When he came home, she was already dressed, bags packed.

"What's all this?" he asked, confused. "Are we going somewhere?"

"Yes, bubba," she said brightly. "A road trip—to Udaipur. We'll be back tomorrow."

"What... I had no idea," he replied, still processing.

"It's fine. Now you do," she said, smiling. "Let's go."

The surprise caught him off guard—in a good way. He needed the escape more than he realized. As he drove along the highway, he glanced at Ruchika beside him, her face lit with joy and affection. And then it hit him—the guilt. Heavy. Immediate. Almost suffocating.

He couldn't fully name it. Maybe it was regret. Maybe it was fear. Or maybe it was the faint trace of Aimee still clinging to him, a reminder of everything that had unfolded over the past few weeks.

Despite their efforts to maintain the fragile boundaries they had set, the emotional undercurrents between Aarav and Aimee continued to intensify. It felt like standing at the edge of a riptide—both aware of the pull, both pretending the water was still.

Their connection, once rooted in friendship and shared history, had shifted into something heavier, messier, and far more complicated.

Aimee had always been deeply attuned to emotions—her own and everyone else's. Her anxious-preoccupied attachment traced back to a childhood marked by inconsistency, where love felt conditional and abandonment always hovered close. For her, relationships weren't just about affection; they were about survival. Closeness wasn't optional—it was necessary. Intimacy quieted her inner chaos, and reassurance felt like oxygen. Without it, she spiraled—overthinking, doubting, searching endlessly for proof that she mattered.

Aarav existed in the opposite emotional current. His avoidant attachment wasn't something he openly acknowledged—not even to himself. Somewhere along the way, especially during his time in New York, vulnerability had begun to feel dangerous. Emotional expression was often met with indifference or criticism, teaching him to withdraw, to protect, to detach. Needs—his own or anyone else's—felt like liabilities. It wasn't that he lacked feeling; it was that he no longer trusted what those feelings could cost him.

Reflection

Sometimes the most painful connections are not built on betrayal, but on misaligned wounds—where one person reaches for closeness to survive, and the other retreats to stay safe. In that space between need and fear, boundaries blur, intentions fracture, and love becomes something both people want—but in ways that can never quite meet.

Chapter 78

Their dynamic was almost tragically textbook. Aimee sought connection with the urgency of a drowning woman reaching for a lifebuoy, as though she had slowly become the version of Aarav he once was during their dating days. Aarav, meanwhile, retreated with equal intensity—like a man fleeing a fire he didn't know how to extinguish. They circled each other endlessly, close enough to feel the heat, distant enough to avoid full ignition.

But distance did not mean detachment. If anything, it sharpened what remained unresolved between them. Aimee felt every inch of space like an open wound. She read his silences not as self-preservation but as rejection. When he didn't reply to her messages right away, she replayed their last exchange again and again, searching for a misstep. When he canceled plans, she absorbed it as confirmation of her deepest fears—that she was too much, too needy, too broken.

Aarav experienced her intensity as a quiet emotional siege. Her constant need for reassurance—Are you okay? Talk to me—overwhelmed him. He couldn't understand why everything needed to be processed aloud, why every pause carried meaning. Her emotions arrived in waves he didn't know how to swim through, and so he built walls—subtle, silent, and firm. He convinced himself it was for both their protection.

And yet, they kept drifting back into each other's orbit.

There were good days. Moments when Aimee made him laugh—real laughter that loosened something tight in his chest. Times when Aarav saw past the volatility and noticed her vulnerability: the way her eyes softened when she talked about her childhood cat, the brightness of her smile when she momentarily forgot to fear losing him. In those fleeting seconds, something stirred inside him. A possibility. A quiet what if.

But the bad days eclipsed the good. Misunderstandings multiplied. The emotional push-and-pull intensified. Unable to regulate her anxiety in this complicated, fragile relationship, Aimee began keeping silent tallies of every withdrawal. She accused. He deflected. She cried. He shut down. They moved in a loop neither knew how to exit.

It all came to a head on a rainy evening in July.

Aarav had been distant for days—not cruel, but absent in the ways that mattered most to her. She tried to stay composed, tried to seem unaffected, but her restraint was fragile. When he canceled dinner at the last minute with a vague Something's come up, something inside her fractured. She went to his other apartment anyway, unannounced, her heart racing not with anger but desperation.

He opened the door, visibly startled. His expression flickered between concern and irritation.

"We need to talk," she said, her voice trembling.

Aarav sighed but stepped aside, letting her in. The air between them was thick with everything neither had dared to say.

"You've been pulling away again," she said, standing rigid in the center of the living room, as if sitting would make her too vulnerable. "I can't keep doing this. I need to know where we stand."

He looked at her, exhaustion etched into his face. "Aimee, we've talked about this. I told you I can't do this if you're constantly questioning everything."

"I'm not questioning everything," she snapped. "I'm trying to understand what I mean to you. That's not a crime."

"It's not that simple."

"It is that simple," she insisted. "You're either here or you're not."

Silence followed. He looked away.

Her voice broke. "I just want you to want me the way I want you. Is that really too much?"

Aarav didn't answer. But something in his eyes fractured—a flicker of guilt, recognition, maybe even longing. In that moment, they weren't fighting. They were two people staring at the wreckage of a love they didn't know how to handle. And hovering over it all was the quiet weight of Ruchika.

What happened next neither of them had planned.

It began with a touch—hesitant, uncertain. Aimee reached for his hand, and instead of pulling away, Aarav held it. Her lips trembled. She stepped closer. He didn't stop her. And then they were kissing—not gently, but desperately, as if searching for a version of themselves untouched by months of miscommunication and unmet needs.

Reflection

Some connections don't fall apart because love disappears—they fracture because love asks for different things from each person. When one reaches for closeness to feel safe and the other retreats to feel free, desire becomes tangled with fear. In that space, intimacy no longer heals; it confuses. And what feels like love begins to resemble longing for something that can no longer exist in the same way.

Chapter 79

They tumbled into his bedroom, a tangle of limbs and emotion. Their bodies moved in instinctive sync, but beneath the surface, the same patterns persisted—her clinging, his hesitation, her need, his fear. The passion between them was real and undeniable, yet fragile, charged with everything they hadn't said aloud.

Afterward, they lay in silence. Aimee curled against him, her breathing slow and steady as she absorbed the warmth of his body. For a brief moment, she felt calm. Held. Chosen.

But Aarav's thoughts were already drifting—not out of cruelty, but fear. He understood what this moment meant to her. He knew what it would demand of him next. And he wasn't certain he had it to give.

She lifted her head, her voice barely above a whisper. "What now?"

He had no answer.

The days that followed unraveled quietly. Emboldened by their intimacy, Aimee tried to close the emotional distance between them. She texted more, called more, asked to see him again—always in secrecy. Aarav, overwhelmed, retreated. His responses grew shorter, his reasons vaguer. He felt trapped—not by her, but by his own inability to love her in the way she needed. And beneath that, a darker question surfaced: what kind of partner was he becoming to Ruchika? Was he simply a man betraying everyone involved?

Aimee felt the shift immediately. The silence after closeness cut deeper than anything before it. She swung between anger and despair, between blaming him and blaming herself. Had she asked for too much? Expected too much? Would it have been easier if they had never crossed that line at all?

Aarav, meanwhile, sank under the weight of his guilt. He hadn't intended to lead her on. He cared for her deeply—perhaps even loved her in a way he didn't fully understand. But their connection felt dangerous. It demanded vulnerability, commitment, and the certainty of hurting both Ruchika and Aimee—or risking being hurt himself.

Eventually, they stopped seeing each other regularly. Not out of bitterness, but necessity. They needed distance. Space. Clarity. Yet the memory of that night lingered, clinging to them like the scent of perfume on an old sweater—familiar, intimate, and quietly painful.

Reflection

Some bonds don't fade with distance; they linger in memory, shaped by what was shared and what was never resolved. When intimacy arrives before clarity, it leaves behind not closure, but echoes—reminders of connection that felt real, even when it couldn't last.

Chapter 80

What happened that night didn't end anything. It began something—a quiet, dangerous pattern neither of them could resist.

They didn't talk about it afterward. Not really. Each of them labeled it a mistake, a one-time lapse, but their bodies remembered even when their words avoided it. Aimee, despite the guilt, clung to the memory—the way he had looked at her in the half-light, the way his touch had felt like an apology. Aarav buried it instead, sealing it away in a mental compartment marked unresolved.

Still, they kept seeing each other. Aarav knew Aimee would be leaving the house soon, returning to her country, and he convinced himself that staying casual—friendly—was harmless. He was deluding himself, at best.

At first, it happened under the guise of friendship. A casual coffee catch-up. A we need to talk that stretched into long conversations inside Aarav's car, parked in empty lots where no one would recognize them. Every meeting carried an undercurrent—the unspoken awareness that they were drifting toward another mistake.

They didn't need to cross the line again for the tension to exist. Sometimes, just sitting close on a couch in silence felt like betrayal—especially when Ruchika was nearby.

Then they crossed the line again. And again.

It became a cycle. Aimee would reach out when she was spiraling—after a difficult day at work, after scrolling through Ruchika's Instagram and seeing a smiling photo of her and Aarav. Aarav would try to resist at first, ignore the message, convince himself to be stronger. But eventually, he would call back at midnight, his voice tired but gentle. "Are you okay?" he'd ask, as if concern gave him permission to return.

And when they met in secret, the pattern repeated. Conversations grew emotionally charged. Arguments flared. And inevitably, they fell back into each other—lips and limbs tangled in regret and longing.

Ruchika was always there, a shadow at the edge of everything.

Her intuition was sharp, her emotional radar finely tuned. She didn't have proof—but more than once, she came dangerously close.

There was one night Aarav told her he was working late at the office, finishing a pitch deck for a client. In reality, he was with Aimee at a dimly lit bar in an older part of the city, the kind of place where no one they knew would wander in. They were supposed to just talk. But after two drinks and a shared cigarette on the sidewalk, they ended up in the back of Aarav's car.

It was raining. Aimee's dress clung to her skin. His hands rested on her waist, her breath warm against his neck. The windows fogged over—just like the boundaries they kept promising to maintain.

Afterward, Aarav drove home at 2:00 a.m., guilt simmering beneath his ribs like acid. Ruchika was asleep when he arrived, the bedside lamp still glowing. She stirred and asked if he'd eaten. He lied and said yes.

Another time, she nearly walked in on a phone call.

Aarav was on the balcony, speaking to Aimee in hushed tones. He thought Ruchika was out buying groceries. They weren't arguing—not exactly—but the conversation was heavy.

"I can't do this anymore," Aimee whispered. "You can't keep choosing her and coming back to me when it's convenient."

"I'm not choosing anyone," he said, rubbing his temple. "I'm trying to figure things out."

"You already have someone," she said. "Why am I even here, Aarav?"

Just as he opened his mouth to answer, the front door opened.

"Hey! I left my wallet—" Ruchika called out.

Aarav panicked. He ended the call mid-sentence and slipped inside as if nothing had happened.

"You okay?" Ruchika asked, handing him a cold bottle of water.

"Yeah," he said, forcing a smile. "Just on a call with a vendor."

She narrowed her eyes—not enough to accuse, but enough to show she sensed something was wrong.

And still, he got away with it.

The guilt didn't stop him. It simply became another layer of the lie.

Aimee had always known about Ruchika. That truth lived in a carefully sealed corner of her mind. When she saw them together—passing in the apartment, exchanging polite conversation—something inside her twisted. But when she was alone with Aarav, when his hands were on her and he whispered her name in that fragile, broken way, everything else blurred. In those moments, it felt like enough.

Even though she knew it was borrowed.

Reflection

What they mistook for connection was, in truth, repetition—two people replaying the same wound in different forms. Desire kept them close, guilt kept them silent, and neither was brave enough to stop what they already knew would end badly.

Chapter 81

The worst incident came two months later.

It was Ruchika's birthday. Aarav had planned everything carefully—a dinner at a new rooftop restaurant downtown, the best table in the house, a necklace she had once paused to admire in a shop window, and reservations afterward at her favorite dessert café. On the surface, he was the perfect boyfriend.

But earlier that day, he had seen Aimee.

She had called, her voice fractured, saying she was breaking down—that she needed to see him, even if only for a little while. Aarav told himself it would be quick. Fifteen minutes. Nothing more.

She opened the door wearing one of his old t-shirts, her eyes swollen from crying. He stepped inside, and the door clicked shut behind him. They didn't speak. They didn't need to. Their bodies moved toward each other with a familiarity that bypassed language entirely.

They ended up in bed, tangled in a silence so heavy it drowned out everything else.

He left her apartment an hour before dinner with Ruchika. There was no time to go home and change. He arrived late, flustered, blaming traffic. Ruchika noticed immediately that the cologne he was wearing wasn't the one she had given him.

That night, Aimee texted him a photo—a close-up of her lips, still faintly swollen.

Aarav deleted it without replying.

Ruchika leaned over, kissed his cheek, and said softly, "You've been distant lately. Everything okay?"

He smiled and squeezed her hand. "Of course. Just work stress."

But he didn't sleep that night.

The guilt wasn't enough to stop him. Aimee wasn't either. They were locked into this loop together, and neither of them had the courage to end it.

Sometimes they fought—bitterly. Aimee accused him of using her, of only coming back when things were strained with Ruchika. Aarav pushed back, telling her she knew what this was, that he had never promised her anything. The words cut, but they never stayed gone for long. They always found their way back to each other.

It was a gravitational pull—destructive, consuming, magnetic.

Aimee wasn't proud of it. In her quiet moments, she despised the version of herself she was becoming. The other woman. The one who waited. The one who accepted crumbs of affection and renamed them love. And yet, a part of her believed—naively, selfishly—that Aarav still loved her. That she had a claim on him, even if it was invisible to everyone else.

And Aarav—caught between guilt and longing—kept telling himself he could control it. That he could manage both lives, as long as he kept them separate.

But emotional lives don't stay separate for long.

One afternoon, as Ruchika sorted laundry, she found a folded piece of paper tucked into the back pocket of Aarav's jeans. A receipt. A coffee shop nowhere near his office. Dated on a day he had told her he was stuck at work.

She stared at it for a long time.

She didn't confront him that night. She didn't say anything at all. But from that moment on, she started paying closer attention. The missed calls. The deleted messages. The unexplained late nights.

Slowly, quietly, it all began to add up.

Reflection

Deception rarely announces itself loudly. It reveals itself in fragments—small inconsistencies, quiet omissions, details that refuse to disappear. By the time truth demands to be seen, the damage has already taken root.

Chapter 82

S he never caught him.

    Not fully.

Not enough to say, You're cheating.

But her silence grew colder. Her smiles became practiced, brittle.

And Aarav—who had once been so skilled at juggling his worlds—began to feel the walls closing in.

Still, he didn't stop.

And Aimee, knowing she was part of something toxic, knowing she was hurting someone else in the process, still opened the door every time he knocked.

They were addicts—not to the physical act, not even to each other, but to the emotional chaos that made them feel alive.

They didn't realize it yet, but something was about to break.

And when it did, none of them would come out unchanged.

It was a humid Friday night in July when everything finally came crashing down.

Ruchika had been out with her friends at a rooftop bar in Bandra. She hadn't planned on drinking much, but the wine flowed freely, and her best friend kept nudging her to loosen up.

"You've been so tense lately," she said, laughing.

By the time Ruchika checked her phone, it was 12:46 a.m.

No missed calls.

No messages.

"Working late," Aarav had said earlier. "Big deliverable. Might even stay over at the office if it drags."

She was used to the excuses now. They came from him easily, like muscle memory.

Her friends tried to convince her to crash at one of their places, but something inside her buzzed—a sharp, anxious hum she couldn't ignore.

She booked an Uber.

She needed to see him.

Something didn't feel right.

The elevator in Aarav's building was broken, so she climbed four flights of stairs, slightly tipsy, her heels clicking against the concrete, the air thick and heavy around her. She knew he wouldn't be expecting her.

When she reached his door, it was slightly ajar.

She froze.

The hum in her chest turned to thunder. Her first instinct was fear—Was he okay? Had something happened?

But when she pushed the door open, the hallway light behind her cast her shadow across the living room, and what she saw seared itself into her memory.

Aimee.

On the couch. Legs folded beneath her. One of Aarav's old sweatshirts slipping off her shoulder.

Her hand rested on Aarav's chest.

Aarav—shirtless, sprawled beside her, their fingers loosely intertwined, his head tilted toward Aimee with a softness Ruchika hadn't seen directed at her in months.

They didn't hear her at first.

It was the click of her heel against the floor that snapped Aimee's eyes up—and then Aarav's, groggy, disoriented—until both of them froze.

Silence.

Pure, suffocating silence.

Ruchika didn't speak. Her throat had gone dry, her heartbeat roaring in her ears. Time stretched, every second dragging unbearably long. She watched realization crash across Aarav's face—wide-eyed, guilty panic—while Aimee's lips parted in stunned disbelief.

"Ruchika—" Aarav started, sitting up fast, his voice hoarse.

"Don't," she whispered. "Don't even say my name right now."

Aimee stood instinctively, but Ruchika shot her a look sharp enough to pin her in place.

"How long?" Ruchika asked, her voice trembling, still not looking at Aarav. "How long has this been happening?"

Aarav opened his mouth. Closed it.

That was answer enough.

She laughed—a sharp, bitter sound that didn't belong to her.

"Was it just tonight? Or was it also that weekend you said you were in Delhi for the conference? Or the day you said you were sick and didn't want me to come over? Which lie should I start with?"

"I—" He stood now, reaching for her. "It wasn't supposed to be like this."

"Don't touch me."

Aimee's voice cracked behind them. "I didn't mean for you to find out like this."

Ruchika turned slowly, her eyes blazing.

"Oh. So you've been my wellwisher. Good. Just checking."

Aimee's lip trembled. "It wasn't that simple—"

"Cut the poetic bullshit," Ruchika snapped. "You knew he had a girlfriend. We gave you a place in our house. I tolerated his ex under the same roof. And you—" her voice shook with fury, "—you just didn't care."

Reflection

Betrayal rarely arrives with drama. It arrives quietly—through repetition, entitlement,

Chapter 83

"Aimee, go," Aarav said quietly, urgently—the panic in his voice now unmistakable.

Aimee stared at him, shattered. "What?"

"Just go," he repeated, still unable to meet her eyes.

Ruchika laughed again, the sound almost hysterical now.

"Of course. Now you want to protect me? After sneaking around behind my back like a coward for God knows how long?"

"Aimee," Aarav said, firmer this time. "Please."

Aimee grabbed her bag and walked past Ruchika without a word, her face flushed, her hands trembling.

The door slammed shut behind her.

Ruchika's voice dropped to a cold whisper. "So that's how you do it, huh? Send her away so you can fix this with me? Say the same lies, make the same promises?"

"I never meant to hurt you."

She laughed, tears spilling freely now.

"You never meant to hurt me? You've been sleeping with her. Lying to me for months. Do you have any idea what that does to a person? To realize you were the second choice all along? That I've been loving someone who looks me in the eye and lies so beautifully?"

Aarav stepped forward, his eyes burning red. "I don't have an excuse. I don't. I'm sorry."

"No," she snapped. "You don't get to say sorry. You don't get to stand there looking broken when you did this. You don't get to apologize and hope it disappears."

He nodded slowly, his face drained of color. "You're right."

She studied him for a long moment, wiping her cheeks.

"You know what hurts the most? It's not just that you cheated. It's that I felt it. I knew something was wrong. I begged you to talk to me. And you still kept choosing her."

"I didn't choose her," he whispered.

"Yes, you did," Ruchika said. "Every time you replied to her message. Every time you snuck around behind my back. Every time you kissed her and still came home to me. That was a choice."

Aarav slid down against the wall, silent tears falling as his shoulders shook.

"I loved you," she said finally. "I would've done anything for you."

Then she turned toward the door.

"Ruchika..." he called, barely audible.

She paused, her back still to him.

"You'll look for me in her, Aarav. Every time you kiss her. Every time she says your name. You'll be looking for me. But I won't be there."

And with that, she left.

The door clicked shut—final, heavy.

And for the first time in years, Aarav was truly, terrifyingly alone.

Reflection

Some losses don't happen when people leave. They happen the moment trust is betrayed—when love realizes it was never enough to protect itself from choice.

Chapter 84

The door slammed behind her, the sound echoing like a gunshot in the narrow hallway.

Aimee stood frozen for a moment, as if her body needed time to register what had just happened. Her chest heaved, but the tears hadn't come yet—not fully. She felt it before she could think it: that sharp, sick twist in her stomach. Shame. Hot and corrosive, crawling up her throat. Her cheeks burned with it, her hands trembling as she fumbled to unlock her phone.

Her reflection stared back at her in the dark screen—flushed, broken, wearing his goddamn sweatshirt.

He told me to leave.

The words looped in her mind, not softly, not gently. He hadn't looked at her the way he used to. There had been no tenderness. No panic for her. Just urgency—to hide her, to erase her, to scrub her out like a stain from his life.

She hadn't expected that.

She hadn't expected Ruchika to walk in either—though maybe, deep down, she always knew this moment would come. It was inevitable. All secrets rot in the dark.

Her legs carried her forward, down the stairwell, one shaky step at a time. Her body moved on autopilot—one hand gripping the railing, the other clutching her bag like it held the last scraps of her dignity.

By the time she reached the bottom floor and stepped into the muggy night air, the tears finally came. Silent at first. Then violent.

She collapsed onto the curb outside the building, burying her face in her hands as sobs tore through her.

It wasn't just heartbreak.

It was humiliation.

She had been discarded. In front of the girlfriend. In his apartment. Wearing his sweatshirt. Like an intruder in a life that had never truly made space for her.

And what hurt the most?

He hadn't followed her.

Not a single word once she crossed the threshold. No wait. No I'm sorry. Just silence. Just absence.

Her phone buzzed.

She wiped her eyes, a flicker of irrational hope sparking in her chest.

But it wasn't Aarav.

It was an Uber notification: Your ride has arrived.

She had ordered it minutes ago, without even remembering.

She climbed into the backseat, still trembling, tears slipping quietly down her cheeks as the driver politely looked away. The city blurred past the window—streaks of gold and grey—as her thoughts spiraled, loud and merciless.

What did I think would happen? That he'd leave her for me? That we'd fix everything and start over, like none of it mattered?

She hated herself for still wanting him.

Even now.

Even after this.

She gave the driver Aarav's apartment address—and then the realization hit her.

She could never go back there.

It wasn't home. It never had been.

Where would she go at this hour? She didn't even have all her belongings. She tried booking a flight—once, twice, again—each attempt ending in failure.

Eventually, she gave up.

And ended up at a small, unfamiliar Airbnb, alone with the weight of what she had lost—and what she had never truly had.

Reflection

Sometimes the deepest pain isn't rejection—it's realizing you were only ever welcome in someone's life as long as you stayed hidden.

Chapter 85

S he dropped her bag on the floor and slid down against the wall, legs folding beneath her, forehead pressed to her knees. It was a position she knew too well—her version of rock bottom.

She sat there for what felt like hours.

And then the anger came.

It always followed the sadness. Like clockwork.

Aimee stood abruptly, her movements sharp and unsteady, grabbing the nearest object—her old diary. A photograph slipped out. It had been taken on his old DSLR. She was laughing. He wasn't looking at the camera; he was looking at her. A genuine, stolen moment, unguarded and real.

She didn't hesitate.

She threw it into the bin.

Then she broke.

She cried until her eyes were swollen and raw, until her throat ached and her chest burned. And then it hit her—a sudden, icy chill down her spine. Her hands began to tremble violently.

Another panic attack.

Only this time, Aarav wasn't there to hold her.

She collapsed onto the floor, sobbing, gasping for air, praying for him to come back—knowing even as she begged herself that he wouldn't. Not this time. Not ever again.

Her breathing grew frantic, tears still streaming as her voice rose into hoarse, broken cries.

"How dare you," she muttered into the empty room.

"How fucking dare you tell me to leave. After everything."

The room spun.

She stumbled into the kitchen and poured herself a glass of water with shaking hands, then set it down untouched. She opened a drawer and stared at the bottle of wine she had saved.

She considered it.

Really considered it.

But something inside her screamed, not this time.

Instead, she grabbed her phone.

No messages.

No missed calls.

Nothing.

She typed:

You didn't even come after me.

Deleted it.

Typed again:

I was always disposable to you, wasn't I?

Deleted that too.

Her fingers hovered over the screen. She wanted to hurt him. To rip him open with words. To make him feel even a fraction of what she was feeling.

But what would it change?

So she opened her Notes app and wrote everything she would never send.

Unsent Note to Aarav

You looked me in the eyes tonight and told me to leave.

You didn't protect me. Not from her. Not from yourself. Not even from me.

I let you lie to me. I let you take pieces of me you didn't deserve. I believed you every time you said it was complicated, every time you held me like it meant something.

And maybe it did.

But it didn't mean enough.

Because you chose silence. You chose her comfort over my chaos.

I thought our history would save us. That love—or whatever this was—would be enough.

But you told me to leave.

And I did.

And this time, I won't come back.

She stared at the words for a long moment, then locked the screen.

She didn't sleep that night.

She curled up on the couch, eyes swollen, heart hollow, chest aching in that deeply specific way that only comes when you realize you were an afterthought in a story you helped write.

Somewhere between four and five in the morning, she finally passed out—not peacefully, but from sheer exhaustion.

And when she woke up, something had shifted.

The pain hadn't disappeared.

But it had sharpened.

Focused.

She didn't know what she was going to do next.

Only that something inside her had finally stopped begging.

Reflection

Sometimes the moment you stop waiting to be chosen is the moment you begin choosing yourself.

Chapter 86

S he stared at the words for a long moment, then locked the screen.

She didn't sleep that night.

She curled up on her couch, eyes swollen, heart hollow, her chest aching in that deeply specific way that only comes when you realize you were an afterthought in a story you helped write.

Somewhere between four and five in the morning, she finally passed out—not peacefully, but from sheer exhaustion.

And when she woke up, something had shifted.

The pain hadn't left.

But it was sharper now. Focused.

She wasn't sure what she was going to do next.

But for the first time in a long time, she knew exactly what she wasn't going to do.

Wait for him.

It was nearly three in the morning when Aarav stumbled out of his apartment, the night soaked in silence and smog. The air felt heavy—maybe with monsoon, maybe with regret. He couldn't tell anymore. Everything blurred together.

His phone buzzed again and again in his pocket, but he didn't look.

Probably messages from friends who had seen Ruchika's story—a black screen with a single line:

Goodbye, Aarav.

She hadn't blocked him.

She had simply left.

No dramatic exit. No confrontation. Just the quiet, devastating finality of walking away and meaning it.

He hadn't cried when she slammed the door.

But the tears came now—hot and bitter—as he collapsed into the driver's seat of his car, the keys slipping in his damp grip. The engine roared to life, its low growl barely drowning out the pounding in his chest.

His vision swam. The sharp taste of whiskey still lingered on his tongue—leftover from the half-empty bottle he'd drained in the past hour. He knew he shouldn't be driving.

But staying still felt unbearable.

He needed to move.

Needed to outrun himself.

The roads were nearly empty as he sped down the Western Express Highway. Streetlights streaked past like fractured memories, each one flashing a different regret.

He saw her face in all of them.

Ruchika—looking at him not with rage, but with the kind of heartbreak that comes from profound disappointment.

And then Aimee.

God, Aimee.

The way she had folded into herself when he told her to leave. The way she hadn't argued. Hadn't begged. Had simply gone.

He had never meant to hurt either of them.

But maybe that was the problem.

He had never meant anything.

And now he had lost both.

A horn blared suddenly as he drifted too far into another lane. He jerked the wheel, heart slamming against his ribs.

Overcorrected.

It happened in seconds.

The tires skidded across rain-slicked asphalt. The car fishtailed violently. Metal screamed. Glass exploded.

And then—

Black.

Reflection

Sometimes the cost of avoiding truth is losing everything at once.

Chapter 87

T hree Days Later

The rhythmic beep of machines was the first thing he heard when he came to.

Aarav blinked against the harsh white lights of the hospital room, his head pounding, every muscle in his body aching as if he had been pulled apart and stitched back together with wire. His vision cleared slowly.

And then he saw her.

Aimee.

She sat in a plastic chair beside his bed, a faded hoodie pulled tight around her frame. Her eyes were swollen, rimmed red, a paper cup of coffee cradled between her hands. She looked like she hadn't slept in days.

He tried to speak. Only a croaky whisper came out.

"Aimee..."

She stood instantly, setting the cup aside and rushing to his bedside.

"You're awake," she said, her voice cracking with relief and exhaustion. "Thank God."

He attempted to sit up and immediately winced.

"What happened?"

"You crashed your car," she said softly. "Drunk. Around four in the morning. Three broken ribs, a fractured wrist, and a mild concussion."

"Fuck," he breathed. "Ruchika..."

"She's gone," Aimee said flatly. "She left. She called your sister and asked her to take care of everything. She couldn't come."

A heavy silence settled between them.

"Why are you here?" he asked quietly.

Aimee looked down, then back up, her eyes glassy.

"Because I still care. Even after everything. I hate myself for it—but I do."

Aarav opened his mouth, then closed it again. There were no words left that hadn't already done damage.

She sat back down.

"I've been sitting here for three days wondering what the hell we've been doing, Aarav. For the past year. You and me. This... mess." Her voice trembled, but she didn't stop. "It wasn't love. It felt like love sometimes, but it wasn't."

He turned his face away, guilt flooding him.

"We broke people," she continued. "We broke ourselves."

Six Months Later

Mumbai, India

The sun melted like gold over the Bandra skyline, casting long shadows across the pavement as traffic hummed in the distance.

The evening breeze was gentle, carrying the scent of sea salt and roasted corn from nearby vendors.

Ruchika stood at the edge of the Carter Road promenade, her scarf fluttering lightly behind her, her hand laced tightly with someone else's.

He stood beside her—tall, calm, steady—laughing softly at something she said, his fingers brushing the back of her hand in that unconscious, familiar way people in love tend to touch.

From a distance, they looked like the kind of couple you'd photograph without asking. Serene. Intimate. Like a promise kept.

He leaned down and kissed her temple as they watched the waves crash below.

And for a brief moment, you might have thought it was Aarav.

But it wasn't.

This wasn't a storybook reconciliation. This wasn't the movies. This was real life.

And in real life, sometimes the person who breaks you doesn't get to help you heal.

Reflection

Closure doesn't always come from going back. Sometimes it comes from moving forward without looking over your shoulder.

Chapter 88

Six Months Later

Mumbai, India

The sun melted like gold over the Bandra skyline, casting long shadows across the pavement as traffic hummed in the distance. The evening breeze was gentle, carrying the scent of sea salt and roasted corn from nearby vendors.

Ruchika stood at the edge of the Carter Road promenade, her scarf fluttering lightly behind her, her hand laced tightly with someone else's.

He stood beside her—tall, calm, steady—laughing softly at something she said, his fingers brushing the back of her hand in that unconscious, familiar way people in love tend to touch.

From a distance, they looked like the kind of couple you'd photograph without asking. Serene. Intimate. Like a promise kept.

He leaned down and kissed her temple as they watched the waves crash below.

And for a brief moment, you might have thought it was Aarav.

But it wasn't.

This wasn't a storybook reconciliation. This wasn't the movies. This was real life.

And in real life, sometimes the person who breaks you doesn't get to help you heal.

Reflection

Closure doesn't always come from going back. Sometimes it comes from moving forward without looking over your shoulder.

Meanwhile, in a quiet suburb, Aimee and Aarav were on paths that slowly curved back toward each other.

Both had spent the past six months in therapy, rebuilding from the wreckage they'd left behind. Aimee immersed herself in pottery and group workshops on emotional resilience, learning to sit with discomfort instead of running from it. Aarav found his way back to himself through writing—sharing poetry online, leading small literature discussion groups, learning how to stay present without hiding behind silence.

They hadn't spoken. Not once.

Until one evening at a community open-mic poetry event in Khar.

Aarav took the stage first. He read a piece titled Fragments—about loss, about mistakes, about showing up even when grace feels undeserved. His voice cracked in places, unpolished and raw, but honest. The room listened.

Aimee was in the audience.

Something in his words unsettled her—not painfully, but recognizably. When his reading ended, she felt herself moving forward before she could think twice. She went on stage and read a short prose piece about starting over:

"I was a story I kept repeating until I rewrote myself."

Their vulnerability lingered in the room like fragile glass—transparent, sharp, impossible to ignore.

Afterward, they found themselves standing beneath a streetlamp outside the venue. The silence between them carried memory and regret, but also something new: steadiness. Recognition without urgency.

Aarav broke it first.

"Aimee..." His voice was quiet. "I'm sorry. For everything."

She met his eyes—still wounded, but no longer collapsed inside that wound.

"I know," she said gently. "I've changed. We've changed."

They walked side by side to the nearby café terrace where they had once met, long before everything fell apart. There were no grand gestures. No promises. Just two people choosing honesty over intensity, presence over escape, sitting beneath the same stars where their story had once tangled itself into something painful.

This time, they stayed seated in the truth.

Reflection

Sometimes healing doesn't mean returning to what was.

It means meeting again as who you are now—and choosing, deliberately, whether the story deserves a new chapter.

Chapter 89

They sat across from each other, hands barely touching. The conversation was unnervingly gentle—guarded yet warm, like threading carefully through old wounds with newly learned care.

"How are you?" she asked.

"Rebuilding," he said.

They spoke about therapy breakthroughs. About who they were becoming. About the art they'd created, the boundaries they'd learned to hold, the fears they had finally learned to name without shame.

There was no recrimination. No blame. Just two people who had found their way back to themselves first—and only then, back into the same space. They weren't here because they couldn't let go. They were here because they no longer needed to cling.

It wasn't sudden. But the spark—long dormant—flickered again. In honest glances. In softer laughter. In the accidental brush of fingers across the wooden tabletop that neither of them pulled away from.

When he stood to leave, she reached out and touched his wrist, gentle but certain.

"I'd like to try again," she said.

Not pick up where we left off, but something quieter. Braver.

Let's see if we can become better versions—together.

He nodded, relief washing through him. "Yes," he said. "Carefully. Consciously. Together."

They walked home side by side—not as they once were, but as strangers with familiar silhouettes—moving toward a future neither of them could have imagined six months ago.

Three Months Later

Aimee hosts pottery-for-resilience workshops in a cozy studio in Powai. Her work is soft and bold at once—pieces shaped by patience, grounded in healing.

Aarav runs writing circles, mentors emerging poets, and reads at literary festivals. His chapbook, published quietly and without expectation, sells far better than he ever imagined.

They live in neighboring apartments. Weekends are spent biking around the lake or sipping chai on her balcony. They surprise each other with small, thoughtful gestures—her favorite dark chocolate, his sketch of her latest ceramic mug. Dinner plans are never grand declarations; they're consistent, caring, simple.

They've established new rules: transparency over comfort. Emotional check-ins. Space when it's needed. Their past is acknowledged, never erased—but it no longer haunts them.

They laugh. They argue respectfully. They hold hands through disappointment. They listen when the other speaks. They are learning each other again—bruised, but hopeful.

Because in real life,

people lose people when they take them for granted.

And sometimes, they don't get them back—

no matter how sorry they are.

But love—true love—is built on consistency, care, and courage.

Ruchika found that in Veer's steady presence.

Aimee and Aarav rebuilt it—together—through honest growth, trust, and the willingness to risk again.

They reunited not out of need, but choice.

Not because they couldn't walk away,

but because they chose to stay—and grow.

Their love isn't perfect.

It's deliberate.

It's vulnerable.

In real life, happy endings aren't guaranteed.

But sometimes, they happen—

when two people rebuild, risk,

and finally become the people they needed to be in the first place.

Epilogue

"In the end, love didn't save them from themselves—it waited until they learned how to stop destroying what they were trying to keep."

Acknowledgements

This book would not exist without the people who stood beside me in silence, patience, and belief.

To my family, thank you for your unwavering support, for your understanding, and for allowing me the space to feel, reflect, and grow. Your presence has been a constant source of strength, even in moments when words were not enough.

To those who supported me emotionally, knowingly or unknowingly, during times of confusion and self-discovery—your kindness mattered more than you may realize. Some of you offered comfort, some offered distance, and both played a role in this journey.

To everyone who has struggled with attachment, anxiety, or the fear of being too much or not enough—this book is for you. Your experiences are real. Your feelings are valid. And healing, though quiet, is possible.

Finally, thank you to the reader for holding this story. May you find pieces of yourself within these pages, and may they guide you gently toward understanding, compassion, and peace.

— Anuj Kumar

www.ingramcontent.com/pod-product-compliance
Lightning Source LLC
Chambersburg PA
CBHW022026120726
47901CB00008BA/2443